Bertie's Golden Treasure

Hetty St. James

Cerridwen Cotillion

What the critics are saying...

"Rich in characterization and hearty in emotion" ~ *Romance Reviews Today*

"I adored this story! It certainly kept the reader on edge" ~ *The Romance Readers Connection*

"The forays into society and the pomp and circumstance of the time are so realistically depicted I felt as if I was in the midst of it all. [...] I highly recommend reading Bertie's Golden Treasure." ~ *Fallen Angel Reviews*

"The plot was fresh [...] makes for a very good read which I recommend wholeheartedly." ~ *The Romance Studio*

"I think the writing in this story is outstanding and the pace is fast moving and never stale. The characters are all well thought out and well written [...] I enjoyed every second of Bertie's Golden Treasure and recommend it to all!" ~ *Two Lips Reviews*

A Cerridwen Press Publication

www.cerridwenpress.com

Bertie's Golden Treasure

ISBN 9781419957017
ALL RIGHTS RESERVED.
Bertie's Golden Treasure Copyright © 2007 Hetty St. James
Edited by Helen Woodall.
Cover art by Lissa Waitley.

This book printed in the U.S.A. by Jasmine-Jade Enterprises, LLC.

Electronic book Publication July 2007
Trade paperback Publication November 2007

Cerridwen Press is an imprint of Ellora's Cave Publishing, Inc.®

About the Author

෨

Having the books of Georgette Heyer and Agatha Christie as companions while growing up in the midwestern U.S., it's hardly to be wondered at that Hetty St. James would become a devoted Anglophile. When she decided to write a book, of course it was a Regency novel that emerged. Several others followed, although not all of them to the completed stage. Thanks to Cotillion, however, they soon will all be finished! And possibly even published! Other favorite eras of history are the Plantagenet/Tudor years, but always, Regency is at the top of the list.

In addition to writing and reading about the Regency, Ms. St. James greatly appreciates classical music and Colin Firth as Mr. Darcy. Of course, he was also wonderful as Jack in the recent filmed version of 'The Importance of Being Earnest'. Although once married, Ms. St. James is now not married, but is still the mother of one son, who encourages her writing efforts.

Hetty welcomes comments from readers. You can find her website and email address on her author bio page at www.cerridwenpress.com.

Tell Us What You Think

We appreciate hearing reader opinions about our books. You can email us at Comments@EllorasCave.com.

BERTIE'S GOLDEN TREASURE

ဆ

Dedication

ଛଠ

To the memory of Roberta Hubbard, the first person to laugh at Bertie's antics and to encourage me to continue writing. And to my daughter, Kristen, who couldn't believe I really did it – and continually pushed me into doing even more!

Chapter One

Midsummer's Day, 1812. Kent, England

ဆာ

The circus interested me not at all and I did try to cry off from going. But my dear twin, Bessie, pleaded with me to come along. "Bertie, surely you don't want to miss the opportunity to see wild animals you may never be able to see again?" The aunts also importuned me to enjoy a "nice day away from home, dear," further eroding my objections. However, despite Bessie and the aunts and all their joint persuasiveness, it was finally and truly only the presence of Sean Brett that won over my misgivings and persuaded me to go to the circus. Just as he had, without even being aware of it, influenced nearly all of my actions during that golden summer and perhaps even for the rest of my life.

Contrary as usual, I refused to dress up for the occasion, being of the opinion that comfort is of far more importance than style. Furthermore, I didn't want to give Sean the notion that I thought his presence was important to me, even though it was. At ten and six years, one is seldom outwardly sensible and logic was not yet necessarily anything to which I greatly aspired. I chose to wear a rather faded muslin dress which had long been one of my favorites and should have been discarded long before, but that I could not bear to part with it. A pair of half boots on my feet in the anticipation of much walking around the grounds completed my unfashionable toilette.

Even though we are twins Bessie and I had always been the exception to that old saying "as like as two peas in a pod." Bessie will always be tiny whereas even then, having just attained the age of ten and six, I was already nearing six feet in my bare feet.

Bessie has a halo of short reddish curls that suits her perfectly no matter where she is or what she is doing. My long, thick, straight, always unmanageable chestnut-colored hair was, as usual, hanging down my back, restricted only by a ribbon that would have matched the original color of my now faded muslin. To the dismay of the aunts I refused to wear a bonnet although I did carry a sunshade. The poor old dears were aghast at the way my face was exposed to all weather and it had already, by the middle of the summer, assumed a rich golden hue that I thought a very becoming contrast to my hair color, as well as a warm frame for my brown eyes. Such golden skin is the opposite, so I've been told, of fashion. The aunts tried to do their best but I found it hard to believe that a sickly looking lily-white pallor could be the epitome of beauty. They continued to persistently warn of freckles—and worse.

There was great excitement in the air as Bessie and I set out in the carriage. This was greatly against her will, as she was on this day wearing a dress which prevented her from riding astride as she usually did. Much to her disgust our younger brother Tyler and his friends were mounted and I thought we made an impressive cortège. There were Tyler, Anthony with his blue, blue eyes and Simon with his flaming hair on one side of the carriage, with Sean—he of whom I dreamed every night—Gareth of the bashful smile and Harry on the other. Harry showed to very good advantage while riding because one could not tell that he had a limp.

Bessie chattered incessantly in anticipation of this spectacular event. But then, Bessie was always outgoing and had always made friends easily. I was almost painfully shy. We were both blessed with pleasing feminine curves— proportioned properly to our respective heights at least— although Bessie's were sometimes hard to discern, clothed as she nearly always was in disreputable old breeches and jacket. The aunts complained that mine were also hard to discover as in addition to the tendency to slump in an attempt to disguise my height, I further tried to disguise my size by wearing too-large, frequently baggy clothing.

The short trip to the circus field was a musical one. Trees along the roadway were noisy nests of birdsong. Beside and in front of us the harness jangled and creaked and under it all the hooves of the horses thudded against the dusty ground, occasionally striking sparks from the kicking of a stone. All of these lovely sounds however took second place to the words that ran rhythmically over and over through my head—Sean Connor Carruthers Brett.

Even though I had had nothing to say about these plans, I could not be other than pleased with them, for Sean rode on Bessie's side of the carriage. This meant that whenever I turned to talk to her, which was for most of the too-short journey, I could not help but see him out of at least the corner of my eye. Even though he was somewhat older than Tyler, they had been friends at school. I had secretly loved Sean devotedly since the first time I had laid eyes on him, three summers previous to this one. That was when he had first accompanied my middle brother Jonathan on a repairing lease to the country. I loved all six foot plus, of him. He is the largest man I have ever seen, larger even than Zeke, our village blacksmith, who is easily able to look down on my brothers, a very rare occurrence in our lives!

Four hundred years earlier Sean would most likely have been executed for having too close a resemblance to the young Henry VIII for comfort's sake. Even so, Sean was tall and broad with longish, curly blond hair and, in defiance of the current fashion, a full beard and mustache. I think it was this that first caught my eye, as I had never seen a man with hair all over his face. Mostly, he pulls his blond curls to the back of his neck and ties them with a black silk ribbon as men did in the previous century and perhaps even still do in Ireland, which is where his family estates are. Oh how I longed to be that ribbon!

He reminded me of a pirate king. In my fancies I dreamed that he rescued me from whatever pitfalls a foolish young lady of my station in life would find herself. The fancy always ends with the rescue, during which he holds me in his strong arms and kisses me as he confesses his undying love for me. And then I always wake up. But I care nothing for reality so long as I might just continue to dream of Sean and relive in my mind those occasions when he would wink at me, or offer an outrageous morsel of flattery, to which I must admit that I was highly susceptible.

As we neared the village I was surprised to see banners and placards hanging from the trees. Gaiety was so thick in the air you could almost feel it. I sighed and tried to prepare myself for what I was sure would be a boring day. Sean would most certainly concern himself only with the young men, not with me, whereas he was the sum and substance of my concern.

The weather could not have been more splendid. Not too warm or too cold and with no sign of rain. The sky was an improbable cerulean blue, with here and there immense fleecy white clouds drifting lazily from west to east. At least, I thought with a sigh, I would be able to enjoy being out-of-doors on such a perfect day.

We had brought our groom Tom with us to care for the horses and the carriage. When we arrived at the circus grounds, Tyler was adamant that not for one moment should Tom be so distracted by his surroundings as to forget why he was there. I saw the glitter of a gold piece as it passed from Tyler's hand to his to ensure his attention.

We set out—a jubilant, noisy group of happy young people—to inspect the attractions. In spite of my qualms, I soon became caught up in the high spirits of the others and began to enjoy myself. Just inside the gateway to the grounds Gypsies whirled around in dances accompanied by a fiddle and a tambourine. We stopped for a few moments to watch them. Never have I seen dancing such as theirs. Simple stories of love and anger were told with their twirling yet sensuous movements and flashing eyes. When one young man mimed the slaying of another with his dagger, the audience drew in its collective breath, releasing it only when the "slain" young man rose to his feet to accept the boisterous applause.

The dusky young woman who had been shaking the tambourine then turned it over and used it for a collection plate as she passed among the watchers, bestowing a smile that varied greatly according to the size of the contribution and, I thought ruefully, the attractiveness of the contributor. Tyler, of course, received the most radiant smile of the ones she happily bestowed.

There was a puppet show and a dazzling display of jugglers, mimes and a stilt-walker who towered over even me! And, amazingly, I discovered that I was enjoying myself. A young woman dressed in the costume of a London pie-seller from two hundred years ago, walked through the crowds selling meat pies which, by their delicious smell, were not more than twenty minutes out of the oven. We bought her entire supply! Along with several jugs of fresh country ale they provided a wonderful picnic under the shade of the large oak tree bordering the meadow site of the circus.

Simon and Anthony suggested that it seemed an appropriate time for a nap but Bessie was anxious to resume our tour. There were still to be observed a daring acrobatic riding demonstration and the wild animal display. But most especially not to be missed was the fortune-teller.

This latter attraction held the most immediate fascination for Bessie. She grabbed my hand and fairly danced around me, crying, "Come Bertie, let us go to see what is going to happen to us!"

"I know what is to happen to me. I do not need to visit the fortune-teller for that," I protested. "And, as near as can be, I know what is to happen to you as well."

Sean rumbled, "I thought all young ladies wanted to hear about the tall, dark and handsome young man who will soon cross their path? After, of course, you have crossed the palm of the gypsy with silver or gold." Lazy laughter from the other young men accompanied this statement. I avoided looking at Sean.

"I am not at all concerned about any young man crossing my path, even if he be short, fat and with a squint," I replied carelessly, while at the same time, thoughts of a certain tall, blond giant flittered through my mind. I felt my face becoming rosy and hoped no one noticed. I turned away.

"Oh Bertie, you must come too!" Bessie said with a giggle.

"I must?" She was in such a happy state, there was nothing I could do but capitulate with good grace. "Let us go then and be done with the nonsense."

Tyler spoke up. "We will just accompany you and then go on to the rest of the circus." He looked at his fellows. "Never can tell what we might see." He turned his head to follow with his eyes the meandering path of a girl who was looking back over her shoulder at him. I could not help but laugh at him. I fear that my beloved scapegrace brother Tyler will never change.

The gypsy's tent was festooned with all manner of scarves and colorful signs of the zodiac were painted around it at random. A darkly handsome young lad stood outside the tent. As we approached, he said, "Ah, pretty ladies, Madame Zorina can say what lies ahead in the years to come. She will tell you things you have never even dreamed of." He looked from Bessie to me. "Which of you pretty young maidens wishes to be the first to discover the mysterious secrets that only Madame Zorina knows?"

Bessie jumped up and down, clapping her hands. "Ooh this is famous!" she exclaimed. "Bertie, do let me go first!"

As I didn't care if I never went in, letting Bessie have the first turn was no hardship. I sat down under a nearby tree to wait for my turn. I placed no faith in such things but I knew I must go along or spoil the happy mood of my companions.

The sound of the Gypsy fiddler carried through the soft air, mingled with the cries and yells of the participants in the games. Occasionally the whinny of one of the trained horses would be followed by the roar of one of the wild animals. It was a strange medley of noises but a not altogether unpleasant one. Simon and Anthony sat down, one on either side of me and we waited for Bessie. Tyler, Sean, Gareth and Harry wandered off together.

It seemed a long time before Bessie came out of the Gypsy's tent. Or rather I should say she "floated out" and over to where we sat. "Bertie, she really is very good! She told me I am to be married —"

"Well that is no great surprise. It —"

"Yes but how can she know that his hair is to be like a fire?" All eyes immediately turned to Simon, whose face suddenly matched the color of his hair. "Or," she continued, "That someday I should come into a treasure of silver? She could have no other way of knowing those things. Do go and see what she has to say for you."

I entered the tent. It was so dark inside that for a few moments I was compelled to stand still lest I fall over something. As my eyes became accustomed to the darkness I could just make out the shape of a figure seated at a low table.

A harsh, low pitched voice said, "You do not believe, do you young miss?" I sucked in my breath. The voice continued. "Please to sit beside me. I will light the candle when you are seated." Cautiously I advanced one foot after the other until my foot touched the table and I sank down sideways to the floor. To my surprise, there was a large cushion already placed in the proper place for sitting and I shifted myself into a comfortable position. A flare from a tinder box lit up the tent briefly and then a low light flickered into existence. The light moved slowly to the table between us. I gasped.

Madame Zorina—for so I supposed this creature to be—was a tiny wizened woman with at least eighty years in her dish, who stared at me out of the blackest eyes I had ever seen. They seemed to have no end to their depth and I felt a chill creep up my spine. "I can see for you in any of three ways miss—or all of them if you prefer. I can read your palm, look into my ball of light or use the tarot cards."

I tore my gaze from hers and looked around in the dimness. There was a ball made of glass on the far side of the table. I was entranced by the light emanating from within it, where seemingly every color of the rainbow was swirling around like smoke inside the globe. For all my intended indifference I had to admit that it was most intriguing.

I tried to speak but discovered that my voice had left me. I closed my eyes and took a deep breath. Whatever had come over me? Surreptitiously I pinched myself with one hand in an attempt to stay awake. Finally in a hoarse whisper I responded, "It makes no difference to me."

In a softer voice than the one she used before she said, "Will you then place your hand in mine, miss?"

My hand seemed to have a life of its own as it inched across the table and placed itself trustingly in her little claw. She slowly ran her fingers over the back of my hand and down my fingers, then turned it over and traced the lines of my palm. Her fingertips were amazingly soft and her touch was gentle but still I shuddered unintentionally and was embarrassed. She continued to caress my hand.

"You do not let yourself lose the control, do you, miss?" A curious odor, not unpleasant at all but one that I could not identify, seemed to suddenly invade the small tent. Madame smiled and said, "You have nothing to fear from me." She continued to stroke my hand. "I see that you will have a long life." Ah-h-h at last, I thought. This was much more the thing. I could feel the tenseness evaporate from my body with these expected words. I sat up a little more attentively.

"You do not live what is called a 'normal' life do you, miss?" Her voice was flat with no emotion. "I do not believe however, that you really wish to continue to live as you do. There is a man—"

I jerked my hand from her grasp. "No," I muttered. "No, no. I do not wish to—"

"Miss," she said in a stern fashion, "you came to me. I tell you only what I see." Her tiny, glittering black eyes were once again exerting their magic hold on me. She held out her little hand and to my surprise, my own hand once again found itself within her grip. I felt myself relax as the gentle stroking soothed me. My head was suddenly so heavy I could barely hold it upright.

"There is a very large man, whether or no, miss. He changes much. He chances much also and will present you with a golden treasure."

My head snapped up. I tried unsuccessfully to remove my hand but she refused to release it. "Such fustian! My sister gets silver but I am to get gold! Likely the next young lady who makes her misguided way into this place will get diamonds, or emeralds, or—" I was so indignant I could hardly speak.

"Your sister, miss?" she asked.

"Yes my sister, who was here just before me. She sent me in here. I didn't really want to come." I peered at the old woman through the gloom. "Likely she told you what to tell me."

There was an edge to Madame's voice as she replied, "Madame Zorina does not need to be told, miss. I see what others cannot see. It is that which I tell those who come to me." She was again stroking the back of my hand and the odor was once again noticeable. I wanted desperately to get out of that tent and into the fresh air.

"Thank you, Madame Zorina," I began, "But—"

"I have not yet told you all," she snapped at me. "You will suffer a hurt but it will not be a lasting one and then you will find the mystery of the gold. Remember this. It will help you, until you find the gold. The hurt will not last. You will be very happy." She smiled at me one last time. "Now you may go — unless you wish me to tell you more?"

I tried to compose myself. My muscles did not want to support my body and I was unsure of my being able to rise and walk out of the tent. Then Madame Zorina slapped my hand and instantly I was myself again. I nodded and rose to my feet, turning toward what I thought was the entrance but Madame Zorina motioned in the other direction. I saw a slash of daylight and walked through it, finding myself back out-of-doors.

I blinked in the sudden light and stumbled. Tyler had returned in the meantime and was there to support me.

Bessie smiled and said, "Isn't she wonderful, Bertie? What did she tell you?"

"You may get the silver but I will have gold." Sarcasm crept into my voice. "But only after I am hurt. A wonderful fortune, don't you think?" With these words, I sank to the ground, in defiance of Tyler's arm around my waist.

I looked around for Sean but he was not there. Neither was Gareth. Where could they have gone?

"Hurt?" Bessie whispered. She flashed a look at Tyler that I could not interpret.

Tyler shook his head at her, frowned, then looked at me. "Gold eh, old girl? I say, you will put the rest of us to shame, I think." He sat down beside me and looked closely at my face. "Are you all right, Bertie? You look a little, um, er, not quite the thing. Would you like some lemonade?"

"I just need air. It was stifling in that tent. The odor —"

"Odor?" asked Bessie. "What odor? I didn't smell anything."

"I have never encountered it before today. I have no idea what it might have been, although it was not unpleasant. But it did make me sleepy." I raised my chin and drew in a deep breath. The fresh air did wonders for my head which still felt heavy. Simon leaned down and handed me a glass of lemonade. I looked at it as if I had never in my life seen such a thing, mystified by the little rivulets of water running down its side.

"Come Bertie, drink up. There is so much more to see. Hurry!" Bessie coaxed me.

"I don't think—" I began. Tyler shrugged then patted me on the shoulder. His touch was strangely comforting. Bessie and Tyler were still flashing looks at each other over my head.

"Here now, my girl. Surely you wish to see the riding displays and we have not yet been to the wild animals—" He stopped as if noting the shudder running through me.

The lemonade tasted cold and sweet and I could feel myself becoming more alert. That was it! I felt just as I did on those mornings when I overslept and my head was fuzzy and unwilling to wake up. Taking another deep breath, I looked at my companions. I did not wish to spoil the outing for the others. Perhaps walking around would help somewhat, as it did on those mornings. My sunshade would help. I looked around for it.

"What is it, puss?" asked Tyler.

I answered in some confusion. "My sunshade? I do not seem—"

Simon promptly offered it to me with a low bow, such as a Cavalier would have done with his own plumed chapeau for a flourish. "I have been guarding it with my life, Lady Bertie." There were glints of humor in his eyes as he smiled at me. "It has been regarded as kindly as a token of honor from my lady fair." The others hooted at this preposterous statement, the mood was broken and I felt happy and secure again. I stood up and Simon held out his arm to me. "I shall protect you, ma'am, from the ferocious wild beasts—" He stumbled as Tyler thumped him on the back. Now what was this? There were so many undercurrents swirling about me. I couldn't understand any of them.

I turned to Simon with my most flirtatious smile and said, "I should be most pleased, kind sir." He put up the sunshade, adjusted it over my head, placed my hand on his arm and we joined the others heading for the riding demonstration.

I must admit that I was pleased to see that there were benches placed around the hastily constructed open-air arena where the display was to take place. My brothers and Bessie are all neck or nothing riders. I had been treated to exhibitions of their excellent foolishness through the years but not even that had prepared me for this display!

The cattle were obviously prime and just as obviously knew it. Bridles and harness were all richly decorated with great flashing "jewels", cloth of gold or silver, or with flowers. There were men as well as women riders, singly and in groups. The horses kept to their rhythmic gaits, lifting their great hairy feet as they pranced around in circles, the small humans cavorting on their broad backs. Somersaults were the order of the day, forward, backward and sometimes even sideways in order to land the acrobat on the back of a different animal entirely!

The scanty costumes worn by the riders were glittery with spangles. Both men and women were showing more flesh than was deemed fitting by proper society, their muscular bodies were encased in very tight-fitting clothing. There were no sleeves visible on anyone. I gasped at the brevity of the dresses on the young women. I could not envision ever exposing myself by showing my limbs in such a way. They flung themselves and each other around with great abandon, drawing great yells of approval from the enchanted audience. Occasionally there would be a near miss before the shaky legs of the performer would finally become steady once again and the routine would then continue as though nothing had happened, to be followed by even greater yells and cheers.

I quite forgot my earlier discomfort in my enjoyment of watching the acrobats and was exceedingly disappointed when the performance was brought to an end. But, in truth, I could not think of anything they might possibly do to top their final performance. It was an astonishing display of a triple rank of riders supporting two others on their shoulders and completed by a young woman on the very top.

I turned to Tyler to ask if there was to be another display later in the afternoon and was startled by the look on his face. He was watching me but the look on his face was one I had not seen there before. There was speculation and also some devilry mixed in with it, I was sure.

Bessie jumped up and down, clapping her hands. "Wasn't that the most wonderful thing you've ever seen? I can hardly wait to get back home and see what I may do." Tyler scowled at her.

Simon patted my arm. "And now, ma'am, may I escort you to the exhibit of the wild beasts?"

Bessie sucked in her breath, causing all eyes to turn to her. I caught a fleeting frown from Tyler directed at her and felt a frown on my own face.

What was going on with those two? I had never seen so many frowns before in my life. Except from Countess Joan, of course. But then, our oldest brother's wife is so excessively high in the instep that frowns are her habitual expression. At least they always have been so whenever I have found myself in her presence.

Tyler's countenance cleared. "Well then, let's go to see these 'ferocious beasts', shall we?"

The wild animals were kept on the far side of the meadow, as far away as possible from the horses. We chatted back and forth and laughed as we walked over to the display.

There were any number of cages, some quite large and mounted on wheels of their own. The noise from their inhabitants was a mixture of squeaks, growls and chirps, which somehow blended into a melodious sound. I wrinkled my nose as we approached, thankful that the exhibition was out-of-doors. I could not imagine such a display within the confinement of a building, no matter how large, mingling as it did the various odors usually associated with the stable—and much, much worse!

The smaller animals were at the beginning of the arcade, the first being a pair of monkeys, chattering and climbing around their cage. Some little boys who, I thought, were rather too close for safety, tossed small stones into the cage. They did not seem to be throwing them at the animals but rather to them. I soon discovered the reason for this. As soon as a stone would hit the floor, one of the monkeys would race over to it, pick it up and then throw it back at the boys. This action caused the boys to screech with laughter.

One little tyke did venture rather too close and suddenly gave a shriek as the monkey grasped his hair and gave a good tug. The boy escaped the monkey's clutch and after retreating somewhat, treated the monkey—and the rest of us—to a display of language such as I had never heard before. The men laughed, as Bessie and I flushed and covered our ears with our hands. The keeper came running over and shaking his fist at the boys, chased them away.

The next cage contained a shabby wolf that looked a great deal like a large and unhappy dog. His gray coat was shaggy and lackluster and he lay panting in a corner, not at all interested in us. Bessie had to be restrained from getting too close, as she was sure he was ill. A suspicious glitter in her eyes as she was led away touched me. I knew only too well what she was thinking—a short stay in her "nursery" and he would soon be right as rain.

Another cage was a much larger one. There was a heavy wall built across the middle, dividing it into two separate compartments. The inhabitants of either end were vastly different from each other, as well as from anything I had ever encountered. There was a large sign across the top of one of the wider sides which read, "From the Antipodes." A large and very handsome man of about forty summers stood near to the cage, instructing viewers not to try to touch either animal. We all gathered around him to hear his explanation of these strange creatures.

The man proved to be Major Henry, the owner of the circus, who had once held a commission in the army. He had been assigned to escort transportees to the penal colony in Australia. After fifteen years of service, during which he had become quite enamored with the country, he decided to sell out and returned to England, bringing some of his adopted country with him, represented by these animals.

One of them was a small, cuddly looking thing, covered in gray fuzz and possessing enormous eyes and ears. The Major called it a bear of some variety but it certainly did not resemble any of the pictures of bears I had ever seen. It prompted one to wish to hug it as one would a dog or cat. During the explanation by the Major, it made no noise, only sat there blinking its great eyes and looking sadly out at the strange world in which it found itself.

The other animal, however, was very active and occupied itself by hopping around its cage, supported by a thick tail. It was also gray in color but bore no resemblance to the other Australian animal. It had very small front legs, almost like hands, while its head most closely resembled that of a deer. There was what could only be called a pocket on its front, which the Major called a "pouch" and said that its young were carried around in there by the wallaby—for that was its name—which was a smaller version of the kangaroo.

I was entranced in spite of myself. I looked around to discover that the others were, also. Tyler asked the Major if the wallaby was inclined toward fisticuffs like a kangaroo and was answered in the affirmative, although he also added that he had no plans to allow such activity.

Without any of us having realized it, the sun was sinking rapidly in the west. Abruptly the leaves on the surrounding trees began a furious rustle. The clouds had disappeared, as had the bright blue of the sky. Some of the animals were becoming restless in their cages and it appeared that we might be in for a summer storm.

Simon suggested that if we wished to see the remaining animals we must hurry, or we would certainly be caught in the coming rain. I looked around and realized that Sean was still nowhere around us. Before I could speak, Tyler dragged himself out of conversation with the Major and we continued our inspection. There was nothing as interesting as the two strange Australian animals, just the expected tiger and lion. And then we came to the last cage, placed a little apart from the others.

Tyler took my arm and strolled with me over to this cage. The others became strangely quiet and for some strange reason, I shivered. Tyler, his face expressing concern, asked, "Are you cold, puss?"

"No," I answered and added impishly, "it's just someone walking over my grave, I expect." I was not at all prepared for the startled look that flashed across his countenance and drew back from him. "What is it?" I cried. "Surely, you realize it was only a jest?"

"Of course," he replied with a false-sounding chuckle, leading me on toward the final cage.

For the first time I looked at the creature within, which stood there, calmly looking at us from what appeared to be green eyes. I did not wish to get close enough to make certain and only squinted at it from a distance. Its entire body was covered with the strangest fur I had ever seen. It certainly did seem to be of a perfectly peaceful nature, or at least it was as we stood there watching it. Each of its front paws was wrapped around one of the bars of the cage. It appeared to be at least seven feet tall as it easily stood upright like a man. I saw no sign of a tail. I was repelled, yet fascinated.

The fur was myriad colors, ranging from the red of a fox, to the tawny of the lion, to the dark brown of a bay horse. It was in patches and stripes and spots. Indeed, its fur seemed to be a combination of all these animals, as some of it was short and some of it was shaggy, especially around the head and what might be considered its face.

As I watched the poor thing, a fly must have flown into its eye, because it winked at me. I shrank back in amazement. Its paws began to shake the bars of the cage as a low rumbling sound emerged from its mouth. What on earth was this strange creature? It reminded me of the monsters—half man, half animal—that one dreams about in childish nightmares.

Tyler and the others had pulled back slightly, leaving me standing by myself, closest to the cage. They were talking softly to each other, commenting on the various animals but I could not tear my gaze away from this one in front of me. I noticed that one of the bars seemed to be loose. As I turned to mention this fact to Tyler, we were startled by the sudden boom of thunder and the creature let out a roar. I turned back again just in time to see the bars come loose. The creature jumped down from the cage and came toward us.

With a flash of lightning as warning, the heavens opened and we were thoroughly drenched by the rain before we could begin to run for cover. I turned to run but felt a restraining hand on my arm. It was a fur-covered hand! I screamed and began to run, heedless of my skirts or anything else. I looked back over my shoulder, to see the creature still pursuing me.

I am not ashamed to say that I whimpered as I ran. The sight of that great furry beast pursuing me was enough to give me nightmares for months to come! Where were Tyler and his friends when I needed them? Another hasty look told me that they were nowhere near. I was filled with fear at the thought of the ogre that was now only feet behind me. A stitch in my side began to hamper my progress and my whimpers changed to sobs. I could not continue and turned to face my doom.

But yet another, greater shock was in store for me. The beast, still in its upright position, was near enough to touch. The rain had not seemed to bother the other animals at all but this one...oh my, its fur was coming loose and falling off in great clumps! As I stood gasping for breath, I was in some way compelled to notice that here and there great expanses of a strange and strangely attractive, golden-hued skin showed through these gaps in its pelt. Little clusters of fur had left a multicolored trail in the wet grass as it pursued me.

As the rain continued to fall, more and more of the fur fell away. I stood, wobbling, gasping, staring at my nemesis. My jaw dropped as I became aware of the very familiar-looking ribbon that was dangling from the back of the brute's head and my hand unconsciously reached out toward that golden head.

Briefly, my gaze dropped and, startled, raised itself again. The significance of all that fur lying on the ground behind me penetrated my sensibility. Indeed, so much fur had fallen off the creature that it was exposed to me as a mostly unclothed man!

Realization and shock swept over me and the last conscious thought I had was that the beast was no beast at all, or at least not the animal kind of beast. Now I knew why Sean had disappeared. Sean *was* the beast. And then, proving that the countess was a better teacher than she had ever thought she was, I followed her sterling precepts. I swooned.

Chapter Two

February, 1817. Kent, England

෨

"Bertie, whatever are you doing up here? The aunts have been looking all over for you." With too much haste I thrust the book I was reading in the direction of my pocket.

Bessie stood in the doorway, dressed as usual in breeches, loose shirt and boots, her curls in wild disarray. I hadn't heard her approach. "Ooh, it's so hot up here! How can you stand it?" She fanned her face with her cap, stirring up little dust clouds with her actions. "Oh you. I might have known you'd have your nose in a book!" She strode past me to the window and hastily threw it open before coming back to where I sat on a packing case. "Well?"

It was the first truly warm day of the new year of 1817 and the fresh breezes coming through the open window belied the snow remaining here and there on the ground surrounding the house at Hadleighwoode. It was the kind of day that renews your confidence in the world and yourself.

Bessie looked up at me, a questioning look on her piquant little face.

"Oh nothing, really." I nervously pleated the skirt of my gown with my fingers, all of which were dusty from my searches. "I thought to take some of my old things with me to London. I came up here to see if I could find them."

Bessie tilted her head and just looked at me for a moment before she spoke. "What things?"

"Um, my old watercolors and, ah… mayhap a, um, book or two."

"Er." She scuffed one booted foot in the dust on the floor. "Bertie, do you think you might see Sean again?"

"Oh no! Truly no." In my agitation, I jumped up and the journal fell out of my pocket and landed in the dust at her feet.

"What's that?" She reached down to pick up the book. "Why, it's a journal. Whose is it?" She began to leaf through it, beginning at the back. "It's empty. Oh no, here's some writing, up in the front."

"Bessie, do you remember the circus?" I asked, not knowing what to do and hoping to distract her.

"The circus? That circus?"

My throat was so tight and dry I couldn't speak and merely nodded my head.

"I'll never forget it."

"Yes… Well. What you have in your hand, there, is my journal. Sean gave it to me for my birthday that year. The only time I ever wrote in it was just that one day—the day of the circus."

"Oh-h-h." She opened it to the inside front cover and looked at the inscription. Without saying a word, she handed it back to me.

"Tyler and Sean both apologized to you. And I did too."

"But your part was so small. I know I made too much of it at the time but I was so humiliated." I turned away from her and walked to the window. "You wouldn't have turned a hair, being always out at the stables and used to such things. But I was used to being occupied within the house, pursuing ladylike activities. I shouldn't have let a foolish wager overset me so—"

Swallowing a lump of remembrance, I turned back to her. "Sean was the, he—oh Bessie, it hurt so. That he could feel so little regard for me, when I felt so much for him."

Bessie jumped up and ran over to me. Her face was suddenly drained of its usual vivid coloring. "Bertie, did you even then have such a tendre for Sean? And none of us knew. Why did you never tell me? I wouldn't have let them do it, had I known how you felt about him."

"I couldn't tell anyone, Bessie, not even you. I felt like the cat that looks at the king. He was so much older and so handsome—and I was so young and gawky." I laughed, nervously, "Of course, I still am that but—"

"Bertie, you are too hard on yourself," she scolded. "Sean would be fortunate to have you, even now. Especially now."

"I don't even consider that anymore. He never wrote to me. Other than his going off to join Wellington, I know nothing of him."

"Ask Tyler or Nick. They surely know, or know where to inquire about him."

"No," I said firmly. "Sean is the past. I'm going to London and Joan is going to sponsor my come-out and who knows?" I laughed nervously. "The Countess of Woode may indeed have enough countenance to find even me a husband."

We were both silent, thinking. Joan is, well... Joan excels at being a countess. She has had years of practice in such behavior, being the daughter of an earl, as well as the wife of our oldest brother, Nicholas. She is very conscious of her rank and her status as a society hostess of the first rank and an authority on all matters of *ton*. Invitations to her parties are highly treasured. Or so we have been led to believe, not having experienced such events for ourselves.

After the death of Papa, when Bessie and I were just five years old, our oldest brother Nick was under rather a lot of pressure to marry and get an heir to the properties. He went to London to investigate the Marriage Mart, or society, as it is more commonly known. Although it is traditional for marriages to be arranged, matching rank and fortune, Nick insisted that he would first like to marry for love, always providing that love came wrapped appropriately.

It took him four seasons to find the right package. The Lady Joan Smallerton, daughter of the Earl of Henstead, was eminently qualified to become the Countess of Woode. She was an "Incomparable", bang up to the mark in all things. She led poor Nick quite a chase through every bramble bush she could find. Only after nearly a year of this did she finally let him catch her and then consent to become his countess.

I cannot deny that Joan was properly trained for the position and knows the right thing to do—always. She knew for instance, that the right thing to do for Nick's young sisters was to leave them in their own neighborhood but in the Dower House, rather than in their own home, Hadleighwoode, where they might be an inconvenience to the Lady Joan. She did not plan to set up Nick's nursery just yet and what with the involvement of her and Nick at that time with parliament and society, there would unfortunately not be time for the proper care and teaching of two so nearly grown girls, hoydens both.

We were then nine and had no idea we were so nearly grown. Of course, as we did grow older, we then became too young to do almost anything that we wished to do. It's no wonder that we were confused, when we were told at the age of fourteen that since we were as yet hardly out of the nursery, we could not go to London for the Season. However we did go back again for the wedding of our other middle brother Jonathon to his Mary Anne. Nicholas and Jonathon insisted.

As is the contradictory way of things, Lady Joan did begin breeding almost immediately she moved us into the Dower House and herself into Hadleighwoode. I am sure that if she could have found a way to also blame us for these events, she would have done so. However, since she hardly ever saw us, it was evidently too difficult for her to find a plausible reason by which she could hang the blame on us.

We barely saw our first niece Elizabeth, until she was two and by that time considered to be nearly unbreakable. We were not, however, allowed to play with her out-of-doors, as we might get her dirty. When Elizabeth was nearly two, Margaret appeared, followed two years later by Geoffrey and two years after that by Anne. At this point, Joan removed herself to London to the house in Mayfair for part of the year and left the children to the tender ministrations of a nurse, a nanny, a governess, a tutor, a cook, a nursery maid and a footman. I was only surprised that they didn't have their own butler as well.

After having presented Nick with one son and three daughters, she decided that she'd had quite enough of that, thank you and retired to her hostessing duties and her couch.

She has more gowns and fripperies than she can ever possibly use and when they go up to London for the Season, I must admit that she does him proud. With all her lethargy, Joan has somehow managed to retain her figure and when she is adorned with the Woode rubies, she is quite truly magnificent. Fortunately she is a brunette, so they do become her.

After Joan's departure, Bessie and I regularly saw more of the children than did their parents. I feel sure that Nick is not entirely happy with this arrangement but after he took his place in the Lords it was difficult for him to spend as much time at Hadleighwoode as I am sure he would have liked. I must also admit that London is no place for young children.

Bessie's voice penetrated the gloom. "Bertie, don't let Joan persuade you into anything you don't want. Promise? You're wonderful just as you are." Bessie walked over to me and reached up to gently laid her hand on my cheek. "You're the very best of sisters and I love you very much. I'm so sorry about Sean and that circus. I wish we hadn't done it."

"I know," I replied with a smile. "Tell the aunts I'll be down shortly, will you? I will, truly. I just need a little time to compose myself."

Bessie left the room. I sat back down on my packing box, drawn by some compulsion to finish reading, for the last time, about my great humiliation. Not just in front of the man I loved but caused by him. I returned to the past unwillingly but unable to resist, just as one cannot resist running one's tongue over a tooth that has an ache.

Being unable to ignore any book at any time, I again opened the little leather-bound book which had not been opened since that earlier time—an astonishingly horrid day—I had written in it. The inside front cover still carried the youthful and optimistic inscription—"The Private Journal of Lady B., written by Lady Zenobia Hadleigh, sister to Nicholas Hadleigh, Earl of Woode, Hadleighwoode, Kent, England and The World!" Under this grandiose announcement was another sentence, which had, in actuality been there when the book was given to me.

I ran my finger over the words as if to conjure up the writer. I had done this so many times it was a miracle that I had not entirely obliterated them. "Presented to the Lady Bertie in honor of her having achieved her sixteenth year, in the year of Our Lord, 1812, from her devoted cavalier, Sean Connor Carruthers Brett." This last was in a bold, barely decipherable, masculine scrawl. As I turned the page to the beginning of the first—and last—entry, I decided that while the name Zenobia looked quite nice in print, I still much preferred to be called Bertie, the name attached to me in the nursery, as the name Bessie was attached to my other half, Abyssinia.

It didn't take very many minutes to read the five-year-old entry in my journal, once again reliving my humiliation. Not nearly as many hours as the actual event occupied. It had seemed back then to go on for years. If I closed my eyes I could once again see and smell that day. An errant breeze sent a shiver up my back and I came to myself once again, in the here and now.

I held the little book loosely in my hands and sat, staring at nothing. That day seemed to have marked the end of my childhood and the beginning of a period in which I was no longer a child but not yet a woman. I had been so eagerly awaiting my seventeenth birthday, when I would at last be able to go to London for my come-out but after the incident at the circus I wanted nothing to do with men, much less London.

Sean had come to see me the very next day, to apologize and originally I had refused to see him. I wasn't faking when I said that I was too ill to see anyone. The aunts confirmed my state to Sean and to Nick. I didn't even want to see Nick. I was overset not only by the events at the circus but by my own ill-conceived passion for Sean. With the wisdom of five added years in my dish, I can see now that it had been just a prank— albeit a prank that had gone wrong. The prank hadn't been specifically directed at me, even though I was the only one of the Hadleighwoode contingent who hadn't known of it. But I was the one who was humiliated by it and I was embarrassed because of my extreme reaction to the prank. I just could not bear to see the man I loved playing the buffoon.

Nick, however, would not take no for an answer. Sitting on the side of my bed, he gently took one of my hands in his greater one and smiled at me. The tears started afresh, just when I had tried so hard to banish them!

"Well puss. Tell me about it?"

"Oh Nick. I feel such a fool!"

"You feel the fool? There is a very large young man in the parlor who says he is the biggest fool in Christendom. He'd like to apologize to you, my dear but he says you won't see him."

Wordlessly I shook my head. Images of Sean—*sans* clothes or fur—insisted on inhabiting and unsettling my mind. "I can't."

"Sometimes one must do what one wishes most not to do. I really do believe you should let Sean—and Tyler—express their regret directly to you, not just through the aunts or Bessie."

Tyler and Bessie had known all along of my infatuation with Sean. But to be fair, they could not have known that to me it was not just a childish infatuation. I was I believed, at sixteen as much in love with Sean as it would ever be possible for me to be with anyone.

"Tyler has apologized. Over and over again in fact." I felt like a small child snuffling over my problems to Nick as I had done so many times in the past. Nick had been like a god to us, handsome beyond belief, always cheerful and so gentle as to make Bessie and me feel secure, even with his great size. He hasn't changed very much in his basic nature, he only seems subdued sometimes when Joan is busy being the countess.

"And have you truly accepted his apology? Have you forgiven him?"

I could not look at Nick's sensitive face. "Not yet. I can't. He made me a laughingstock Nick, in front of his friends."

"I suppose it natural that you may feel that way but I have seen a different Tyler today. One who gives me hope for the Tyler of the future." He smiled at me and I knew that he was thinking, as I was, of some of Tyler's other pranks.

"He tells me that it was not intended to end the way it did." Nick looked at me steadily for a minute, before he continued. "They did not expect the weather to change the way it did. The glue that they used to cover Sean with the fur lost its power in the rain."

"Why did they do it, Nick?"

"I don't know, puss. One of them, no one seems to remember which one, thought it to be a great lark and bet Sean that he could not successfully disguise himself as an animal and remain in the cage, undetected, for two hours. Never for one moment would Tyler—or Sean—have wanted to really hurt you or overset you. You weren't really hurt were you?"

"Just my pride and my sensibility." I managed a feeble smile.

I had tried to understand. My intellectual side could even accept that it *had* been a wonderful prank but my emotional side could not forgive that it had made me the fool. I didn't think I would ever forget that. Just as I had not forgotten Sean and would not, although I had not seen him since that day.

"I should have liked to see Sean with his fur all coming off, chasing you across the meadow," Nick chuckled and carefully watched my face as he made this statement.

"Well I suppose it might have been funny," I admitted. "Although not to me, not at that time. I was so shocked, so humiliated! For him as much as for myself."

"I will grant you that but then you must grant me my small wish."

"Please don't ask me to see Sean. Please Nick?"

"Just for a moment, puss. And I'll be right beside you. An apology that is offered is obliged to be accepted. Just let him apologize, that is all I ask. You won't need to say anything, if you don't wish to and it needn't take long but he really is remorseful. To please me?"

Whenever Nick asked anything directly of me I was helpless to refuse him. The aunts bustled into my room as Nick left and helped me dress and make myself presentable, then escorted me down to the drawing room. The sight of Sean took my breath away and I nearly bolted back up to the safety of my room. He was dressed as for a court presentation and his hair was neatly bound back. There was not even the slightest hint of a twinkle in his eye as he was totally serious and businesslike. He was everything that was completely proper and dignified to the extreme, this day.

When the aunts left me, Nick stepped quietly to my side, placing one of my hands in the crook of his arm and covering it with his own. Sean approached us, his face like a mask and bowed to me in a very formal fashion. His constant companion, the huge Irish wolfhound Blondel was, as usual, by his side. If Blondel had been with him yesterday I might have recognized Sean all the sooner. I stared at a point somewhere over his left shoulder in order to avoid looking at his face.

"B—" He stopped and cleared his throat, before continuing in a soft rumble. "Lady Bertie. Please accept my most sincere and humble apologies for my actions of yesterday. I am completely ashamed and appalled by my thoughtlessness. It was never my—our—intention to distress you and I would give anything…" He stared at me so intently that he compelled me to look up at his face. Under his breath, so softly that I wasn't certain that I truly even heard the words, he said, "If you were but older." Sean raised one hand and for a fleeting moment I thought he meant to caress my cheek. He glanced briefly at Nick, then at me and lowered his hand to his side. He began again, this time with more emphasis. "Anything to go back to yesterday morning and conduct the day differently. I trust you will believe this, ah, me and find it in your magnanimous heart to forgive me—us."

This was horrible, almost more horrible than what had happened yesterday! It was like watching a mighty oak fall in the forest. I had never wanted to see Sean so humbled, so pleading. This was not the Sean I loved so devotedly. A veritable incomprehensible maelstrom of sensibilities, I gasped and whispered, "No", jerked my arm from Nick's and ran out of the room.

* * * * *

"Bertie! Bertie, are you still up in the attics?" This time the voice belonged to Aunt Cassie.

"Yes, Auntie, but I am by way of coming down now."

"Tessa has come to pay you a visit, dear." Tessa was one of three daughters of the neighboring Squire and the one closest to us in age. She had always been a dear friend. It would seem that Tessa was joining the aunts and Bessie in a conspiracy to disperse my fears about the impending journey to London. If I hadn't been so frightened I might have found it laughable.

I closed the little leather-bound book with a snap. Dust motes took flight from the binding to join those already floating around in the still too-warm, stuffy attic. I could only hope that I had gained in wisdom during the intervening five long, sometimes painful, years since I had written that last entry in my journal. I stood up and shook the dust from my old gown.

I have always been impulsive, rushing my fences and landing in the briars. I believe that there cannot be a more heedless individual on the face of this earth than a sixteen-year-old girl madly in love for the first time. If there is, I hope not to meet such.

I knew I still loved Sean as much now as I did then. So much so, that I knew I would never be able to love anyone else. I had given up on my childish fancies and vowed to accept whatever husband Nick found for me. I would be a good and dutiful wife and mother — this was my most ardent desire. And in time, perhaps, I could forget Sean. I would not be the first woman to enter into a loveless marriage of convenience, nor the last, either.

If one particular dream I'd had three years ago was true, I should have to forget him. As clearly as if I'd held the newsprint in my hand, I saw his name on the list of war casualties. I was so shaken I'd taken to my bed and stayed there for nearly a week before I could come to grips with myself and face anyone other than Bessie and the aunts. I didn't know if it was true or not and couldn't force myself to ask anyone either. Occasionally, we would hear mention of one of the other younglings, as Tyler's friends were called, but never a whisper about the most important one of all — Sean Brett.

Shaking myself out of my reverie and into the present, I concentrated on the reason for my presence in the attic. At long last I was about to make my much delayed and overdue come-out in London. Joan had, at the time of her marriage to Nick, eagerly promised that she would indeed sponsor Bessie and me when the time came for such an event. Her enthusiasm for this venture diminished however over the years, seemingly in direct proportion to my ever-continuing gain in inches.

After several false starts I vowed that this time I would not be put off and had prevailed on Nick to please solve my problem. He did. He found yet another aunt—Kate—who would accompany me to London. There, with Joan's assistance, I might be presented to society, in an effort to make the grand match for which I had been waiting all of my life.

* * * * *

I had come up to the attic on this day to find my valise and hatboxes. As I was to have nearly an entire new wardrobe made for me in London I did not need to pack many of my present clothes but there were some things I needed to take with me. In the first hatbox I opened, I discovered my old journal, along with other treasures and promptly forgot my mission.

Dear Bessie! She had not changed much in the five years, either. In fact, other than the additions to Nick's family nothing had changed, except for me. I had determined that never again should I make such a fool of myself as I had then. It was my own fault that things happened as they did. I had made of myself a perfect target for pranks besotted as I was with Sean, even if no one knew it, not even Bessie. In addition to the fright, my feelings had been trampled and I determined that I would not so soon forget that. The day after I had run from him in the drawing room Sean had sent me a charming posy of very rare, much-prized yellow rosebuds with a note that had one word scrawled across it "Regards". One of the rosebuds, now dried and crumbling, shared space with the note in my treasure box, which I had then carefully hidden away.

Nick, as head of the family, had then sent Tyler off on a disciplinary learning expedition to our estates in Northern England and Scotland. The other younglings dispersed themselves and Sean went back home to Ireland.

Tyler was still the prankster that he had always been but the younglings had been reduced to five now. Sean, the oldest and my sweet nemesis, had joined the army soon after the circus episode and we had not heard from him in the intervening years. We had heard of him, for he had distinguished himself with Wellington's troops and during the war against Napoleon had been mentioned several times in the dispatches for bravery. But he had not communicated directly with us.

I tried to tell myself that I didn't care but I didn't succeed very well. Instead, I'd painted a small portrait of him that I'd then been afraid to show anyone for fear of inciting yet more laughter. I thought it quite like him and for some time afterward had kept it in a pocket of my day dress, carefully placing it under my pillow before I went to bed. Being a somewhat restless sleeper at times, I'd awakened one morning to find the small frame on the floor beside my bed and after shedding a tear or two, had consigned it to the safety of the attic.

Now though, I looked once more at the miniature of Sean and wondered for the thousandth time where he was, what he was doing, if he had married. He had never been listed as having been injured or killed, so I was confident that somewhere he still lived. I would not ask about him but I included him in my nightly prayers. Carefully I tucked the miniature back into its little velvet case before securing it in my pocket and began the descent to my room.

Once there I did indeed find Tessa who was near to bursting with excitement. "Bertie, aren't you anxious to go to London? How could you spend such a glorious day up in those stuffy attics?" She paced as she talked, gesturing with her hands. "I should be counting the very minutes until the time to depart."

"Tessa, how nice of you to come and visit," I responded wryly.

"Poor Bertie, you must be more nervous than usual, to stand so on formality. But if you wish," she paused to sigh loudly, "Good afternoon, Lady Bertie. And how do I find you on this fine day?" She sketched a perfunctory curtsy. I had brought an empty hatbox down from the attics with me. It was still in my hand and I threw it in her direction.

As Tessa is the oldest sister in a family that also includes five brothers of varying ages, she had no difficulty in neatly catching the flying hatbox, after which she collapsed on my bed, laughing. She has such a happy nature and her laugh is of such an infectious variety, I had no choice but to join her.

She sat up, wiping her eyes with her handkerchief. "Oh Bertie, after all your changes of heart and mind, to think that you are finally going to have a come-out. Are you sure that this time you will really go? I shall miss you."

"Joan assures me that the Woode nursery is now complete and therefore she has run out of excuses and so I have quite decided that this time I should go. I do wish you could come with me," I ventured.

"Somehow I can't quite picture the countess giving me houseroom you know," she replied softly.

I laughed at her. "That should not be a hindrance. She isn't giving me houseroom, either. I am staying with Aunt Hattie."

"I enjoyed my come-out excessively Bertie and you will too. You must just think of yourself as an Original and you will be all right-and-tight."

"You have been listening to your brothers and their cant again, my dear Tessa."

She giggled. "I know. And Papa gets in such a pother about it I cannot resist it sometimes. Truly Bertie, you must always appear as though you have behaved with absolute perfection." She giggled again and rolled her eyes at me, "Most particularly when you have not." Standing up, she walked about the room, pausing before one of the windows that looked down toward the stable yard. "Were you not able to persuade Bessie to go with you?"

"I should have been much happier had she been willing to come too." With her size and looks Bessie would, no doubt, set the *ton* on its ear and be a diamond of the first water if ever she could be put into a gown and taken to London for a Season. "Bessie and I were nine when Nick and Joan were married at St. George's in London. It was our first grand occasion and, I think, the first of only three times I have seen Bessie willingly wearing a dress. The other times were Jon's wedding and the day of the circus. But she has absolutely no use for society," I continued. "She refused to come with me, saying she was not a milk-and-water city miss. We've never been parted for more than a day or two and I don't know how I shall go on without her. Bessie insists that I shall go on better without her, since she has none of the gentle accomplishments."

"All of which you quite excel at, casting the rest of us into the shade."

"I do passably I know, but Tessa—"

"Bertie, do not be anticipating anything but pleasant diversions please. If you will but think that you shall have a good time and enjoy yourself, I am sure that you will indeed have a successful season. There is certain to be at least one gentleman in London who will treasure you just as you ought to be, for yourself alone. And it does not hinder your situation at all that you are the daughter and sister of an earl, with an extremely respectable portion."

"But Tessa, I wish only to be—" I could not admit, even to Tessa, my most fervent wish—to be loved only for myself.

"Are you still worried about your height? We've all told you that such worries are nonsensical. Why, I had a stiff neck nearly the entire season, from looking up at all my dancing partners."

"Yes but you have not nearly so many inches as I do, Tessa"

"Bertie, you make too much of it. You will see for yourself. I have not noticed that many married couples dance together anyway. Or at least, not very often. The husbands isolate themselves with other husbands—and the port or whisky—and the wives with other wives and they either talk or play cards."

"It is certainly that way with Nick and Joan, although I have seen Jon and Mary Anne dance together several times. But then, they were a love match and not to be considered by the standards used on others," I answered, deep in thought.

Actually, for all my prating about my excessive inches, it is not at all the prime requisite in my ideal man. I have met several gentlemen with whom I felt that I could have made a successful, if not blissful marriage. They seemed to appreciate my mastery of the gentle arts but fell afoul of the dancing floor. Even my not inconsiderable dowry was not enough to compensate for their eyes being on the level of my chin or my nose. The male ego mystifies me. If it did not bother me, why should they feel foolish because we did not appear to advantage on the dance floor?

"Tessa?" I paused. "What if the patronesses won't grant me vouchers for Almack's? What shall I do then? However will I...?"

"Bertie, they wouldn't dare spite Lady Joan in that way. You shall certainly go to Almack's and many other parties and balls. You'll be an Incomparable!" Now Tessa paused and cocked her head as she grinned at me. "Well maybe not an Incomparable but you will certainly be an Original!"

"Incomparable! Original! Such names mean nothing, except more tattle for the *on dits*. I just hope to have a good time and not embarrass Joan or Nick, the aunts or myself." And all the while garnering the approval of the *ton*, I added to myself.

For without the approval of that *ton*, a marriage for me would seem to be out of the question. I would hope to find love, surely, every young woman does but a sensible arranged marriage might be the best I could hope for. The significant word here being "sensible". Several un-sensible offers had already been made for me to Nick, not a few of them from gentlemen who had never even laid eyes on me! It seemed that the sister of an earl, one of marriageable age, was indeed a prize to be claimed. But Nick was awake on every suit and quickly realized that it was my dowry and not me, that was the ultimate object of their desire.

Tessa's next question made me jump with surprise. "Will your Aunt Kate be there, also?"

"Have you taken up the gentle art of reading minds?"

"No but I could tell by the look on your face that you must have been thinking of her. I know how fond of her you are.

"Yes, she has promised to help with my come-out. It will most likely take the combined efforts of all my aunts, both sisters by marriage and who knows? — perhaps even an Act of Parliament from Nick to ensure my success."

"Bertie, you must not talk so. I declare, you were never used to be such a faint-heart!"

"That's as may be but then I have never had a come-out before, either."

Tessa had appropriated one of my bed pillows and was now dancing with it around my room. "Oh Bertie, I envy you your season. I did so enjoy mine."

"Do you not plan to have another one, then?" I asked.

"Not a season such as you will have. Annette had her turn last year and the next come-out for our family will be a good many years from now when Mary is of age. But Papa has been talking about taking the family to town again. He and Mama enjoy seeing their friends and Mama loves to take advantage of the greater variety of shops. I'm encouraging him to take us all up to town in a month or two, so that I may see for myself what a grand success you'll be!"

"Tessa, you're coming it much too thick! But I do wish I might believe you," I added wistfully. "I wish I might believe in the reality of the Marriage Mart but honestly, Tessa, if a man's wife is his ornament, can you truly imagine me as anyone's ornament?"

"Yes, my friend, I can. Any number of gentlemen should be pleased to have you as such. You will do well, I am certain of it. You must write and tell me everything and I will write back to you. Perhaps by the time you are established we will be in London too!" With those positive words Tessa took her leave of me, casting me even deeper into the glooms.

Chapter Three

March, 1817

ஐ

At last! It was finally going to happen! I, Lady Zenobia Hadleigh, better known to family and friends as Bertie, having arrived at the advanced age of one and twenty, was at last going to London to make my come-out. This time there could be—would be—no obstacles. This time my dream was really going to come true! I was so excited that the aunts—Penny and Cassie, who had raised us—and even Bessie herself, were helping me count the days until I should at last be on my way. That day, they said, peace and quiet should once again prevail at Hadleighwoode. But they said it with love in their eyes and on their faces. Their high expectations for me exceeded even my own.

However, just thinking about the countess and London and all they entailed gave me qualms. I looked around my room at all the things that were dear to me and I wondered if I should change my mind once again and stay here, wrapped in the known and the comfortable. I would certainly miss my home, the servants, the tenants, the neighbors. How could I leave all this for the few months necessary for a London season, let alone leaving it forever? Everywhere I looked there were memories of Bessie and me growing up. On the walls between the long windows were frames containing portraits that I had done of our three brothers, not one of whom resided with us now. Interspersed with the portraits were individual likenesses of our surfeit of aunts. We don't remember our parents.

Our appearance into this world caught nearly everyone by surprise, not least Mama and Papa. They were certain that their nursery was quite complete after the birth of their third son. Mama was by way of being too old, or so she thought, and consequently she just ignored all those strange and interesting feelings she was having, until it became obvious that she could no longer ignore anything and the doctor was summoned. When he assured her that she was indeed breeding, she went into a swoon from which she never really fully recovered. Papa, on the other hand, disappeared into the brandy decanter, emerging only once every two months or so to look around, observe that things were still the same and disappear again.

Our oldest brother, Nicholas, then being twenty and close enough to his majority to assume leadership, did so, taking our middle brother Jonathon, then fifteen and the ten-year-old Tyler under his large protective arms.

You should perhaps know that I am the elder twin, having preceded Bessie into this mortal vale by about twenty minutes. I was large and squalling immediately. Perhaps I should clarify these statements by saying that I have been told all of this many times by Nanny, who was present and is garrulous in the bargain. I do not have any direct memory of these events. Bessie was a puny little thing and scant hope was held for her survival. But she is a tough character to this day and I am sure she survived in great part by dint of her extraordinary stubbornness.

Nanny and doctor found a pair of wet-nurses for us — mine was the larger, of course — and so we grew. Or at least, I certainly did. I do not believe that we have ever been the same size. There are those who claim that one of us is a changeling but there are enough similarities in our character and temperament, that I, for one, do not believe those stories. We are just totally dissimilar in our looks.

Perhaps first I should explain that our given names are not Bessie and Bertie. Papa did appear, I am told, relatively sober at our christening — just long enough to play out his final jest. I am quite certain that it also required several bottles of his best port to ensure the cooperation of the vicar but I cannot prove that. We were christened Abyssinia and Zenobia. I once overheard — and yes, I know all about that old saying about those who listen when and where they should not — Papa explaining our names. Since we were so obviously not planned nor expected, Papa felt that by encompassing the entire alphabet from A to Z, he was ensuring that there would be no more little Hadleighs, as there were no more names available. I do not quite understand such specious reasoning but it is of little import at this late date.

Abyssinia being too much of a mouthful for anyone, it quickly became Bessie. And for some reason I have never ascertained I became Bertie. Unexceptional names, I suppose but ordinary. And one thing we have never been accused of being is ordinary. Our relative sizes would guarantee that if nothing else did. However we are really very close and I treasure Bessie above everyone else in the world.

We more or less fell into this routine when we were still in leading reins. Mama's swoon lasted until we were two years and some months, at which time, she gracefully departed from us while in her sleep. Never one to make a fuss, was Mama. Papa seemed to harbor equal parts of bitterness and anger at us, bitterness because our coming caused Mama's leaving and anger because we were only girls. Perhaps if we had been boys he could have loved us but no matter, he solved his problem by ignoring us. The aunts did their best but had no desire to become real mamas to us and so we each went our own way.

This is why, at our home of Hadleighwoode, we were more or less brought up by Aunt Cassie, the middle of Papa's sisters and Aunt Penny, the oldest sister of Mama. These two ladies, much of an age, had been bosom bows as girls. They had even both been married once, but because of the American War of Independence in one case and an infamous duel in the other, were left widows and so they had come to live at Hadleighwoode long before Bessie and I were even born. After all these years they had become as sisters to each other and are the epitome of dithery dotty old aunts. We love them dearly. Everyone should have at least one such aunt. I am not sure that anyone should have two, however.

Aunt Kate, Papa's youngest sister, lives close to Jon and Mary Anne's Withymoor which is in Somerset. She is my favorite of all the aunts. Partially it is because she is also tall — although not nearly as tall as I am, being only eight inches over five feet. It was the example of Aunt Kate that helped me to be able to stand up straight as I was growing and growing. But there is no question that even she was surprised when finally I appeared to reach my total inches. She is the only one who has seemingly not given up hope that somewhere there is a gentleman who will be taller than I am and who will see me as me.

Aunt Hattie, our papa's oldest sister and also a widow, lives in London and had, on several occasions, been kind enough to invite me to spend some time with her. Of course, since I had not yet made my bows at Court, I could not participate in society by attending any parties or balls other than strictly family events but I was able to visit a museum, a gallery and other sights. At least once during each visit, we would ride in Rotten Row, although usually not during the fashionable hour.

I wished again and not for the first time, that Jonathon and his wife, Mary Anne, could sponsor my come-out. But they were happily and busily engaged with the stud at their country estate and seldom came to town.

Theirs was the marriage that I wished most to emulate, being as it was a true love match. Unfashionable perhaps in society's eyes but highly to be desired in mine. It was fortunate for them both that Jonathon came into a substantial legacy from one of Mother's old aunts, because Mary Anne had not a feather to fly with, being the daughter of an impoverished Scottish earl. She was the former Lady Mary Anne MacTavish, her family's title going back for several centuries.

They both love the land and so are almost completely happy at Withymoor, even though they do not yet have a family of their own. It is a very successful estate and they breed horses. The Withmoor Stud is justifiably famous throughout the land.

Perhaps it was his earlier training as older brother to Jon and Tyler but Nick was always perfectly content to have us follow him around and when our little legs became tired, he would pick us up and with one of us cradled in each huge arm, carry us through the gardens introducing us to various flowers, birds, animals and trees.

For the past five years I had been content to stay at home with Bessie and our Aunts Cassie and Penny. On occasion we were visited by our brothers all of whom are much taller than I am. Of course Nick and Jon both married petite women who barely reach their manly shoulders. Or mine, either.

During this time Joan was also busy fulfilling her duty to the nursery at Hadleighwoode. At last, now that I had reached the great age of one and twenty, there did not seem to be any more reasons for delay available to either of us. This is why plans were now underway for my trip to London.

I had very confused feelings. On the one side were my hopes and dreams for marriage and a family of my own but on the other were my double fears that I would once again be made a laughingstock and, to a lesser extent, my constant feelings of panic when in a crowd. Country society among friends was delightful and I enjoyed it to the fullest but I knew hardly anyone in London. The hallmark of a superior hostess is to hold a ball, or some such function, that is regarded as a crush—by which I mean there are so many people in attendance that it is difficult to move. The more tightly packed it is, the greater the degree of success. I found it hard to breathe properly just thinking about such crowds.

And so now I was finally going to London for my long-awaited come-out, I wished with all my heart that I could accept Tessa's advice as easily as she gave it. I wished with all my heart that I knew what I really wanted. I wished with all my heart that I could know, for a certainty, what had happened to Sean. Would he appear in town, destroying my hard-won equilibrium?

Having been to London before did not mean that I couldn't—and wouldn't—still gawk at the tall buildings and busy streets like the veriest rustic. Aunt Penny chuckled at my renewed astonishment. She had accompanied me on the journey to London and the home of Aunt Hattie. After a few days of shopping and visits to friends and sisters, Aunt Penny would go back to Hadleighwoode, leaving me all alone in London. Well maybe not all alone but without Bessie nearby, I always felt all alone.

Aunt Penny seemed to sense this because she smiled at me and said, "You'll have such a wonder-filled time that you won't even miss us once you get yourself set up with your new wardrobe and all."

"Do you really think so?" I asked.

"That's the way it was for me and for Jenny and always is for every other girl when she comes to town for her come-out."

"Did you and Mama have your come-outs together?"

"No. I was two years older than Jenny, so I'd already made my bows but I came along anyway so as to not miss all the fun!" Her eyes sparkled with remembrance.

"Tell me again how Mama met Papa. Please?" I had heard the story at least a hundred times but I never tired of it. Mama had been Jenelia, Jenny to her family.

"Your Mama was the beauty in the family. She had much the look of Bessie, in size and coloring. She was so graceful and light on her feet, all the young men would line up just inside the door at any party just for the chance to put their names on her dance card." A dreamy smile came over Aunt Penny's face, softening the lines, making her look years younger than she really was. She closed her eyes to help her remember those long-ago events. "We were at a ball at Devonshire House and in walked your papa. He wasn't your papa then, of course but, oh my, what a handsome man he was."

Aunt Penny turned her head toward me and smiled, wistfully. "I think your papa was the walking dream come true of every girl who made her come-out that year and probably several other years as well." She shook her head as she said, "But it made no difference. He took one look at your Mama and that was it. He walked up to her and took her dainty little hand in his big one and after inspecting it carefully said to her, 'I have a ring here in my pocket that I think belongs to you'."

"Jenny just looked up at him, speechless. She'd never seen him before, not ever but she didn't pull her hand away, either. Harry didn't let a little thing like that bother him, though. He calmly reached into the pocket of his waistcoat and drew out the most beautiful ring. It was a very strange ring, made of gold with the top of it encrusted with jewels of all colors and such a very tiny little band."

Aunt Penny was so rapt in her story that she didn't say anything else, until I finally prompted her. "And then?

"And then he slipped that great archaic ring on her finger and of course it fitted her as if it had been made for her. He smiled down at her and said, 'Well that settles that. You'll have to become my countess.' And then he laughed so boisterously, as your Mama just stood there, speechless, looking at that heavy ring on her finger. 'I suppose I ought to seek permission to acquire your hand but you'll have to tell me who you are and where you live before I can do that.' And he just laughed again. Then your Mama started to laugh and, pretty soon, everyone else was laughing too."

"But they did get married."

"Oh yes. Three and a half weeks later. Our father wouldn't allow Harry to use a special license. Made him wait for the three weeks it took to call the banns."

I sighed, as I had every time I'd heard the story. I never got tired of hearing it and doubted if I ever would. It was so romantic and I longed for the same kind of thing to happen to me. "And Mama knew she loved Papa, right from that very first night." I was making a statement but Aunt Penny took it as a question.

"I'm not sure if she truly loved him or if she was simply afraid to say no after that first night. He was the catch of the season, you know and just then our family situation wouldn't allow for another year in town for either of us. I married too, that summer, just a month after Jenny but then my George was killed and I never had another opportunity." Aunt Penny wriggled on the seat of the carriage, changing her position for one that was more comfortable. "Your papa was awe-inspiring in his determination. He never varied in his intentions, either. And I don't think he ever even looked at another woman after the first time he saw Jenny. I shudder to think of what he might have done had she said no."

Now, this was food for thought. Of all the times I had reveled in the story of the mutual love-at-first-sight meeting of my mama and papa, this was the first time I had ever heard that perhaps it wasn't as I'd always imagined it. I would need to think about all of this. But before I could begin to do that we had arrived in London and there were entirely too many things for me to gawk at, so I carefully tucked all my muddled thoughts away for another time.

I soon discovered that Aunt Penny had been correct. Over the next few weeks, I *was* much too busy to feel lonely for anyone or anything. Unless you have been through one yourself, you can have no idea of the turmoil represented by providing one young woman with her entrée into society. I began to feel sorry for Nick and Aunt Kate and have more respect for Joan. She had, after all, been through it once herself and with three daughters and their debuts to anticipate, she surely was wise in conserving her strength. If my debut was any sort of indication of what was to come, several years on her couch should have her in fine fettle.

At the same time as there were constant trips to the dressmakers, the mantuamakers, the milliners and the haberdashers, we must also find the right hairdresser, the right lady's maid, the right dancing master, the right caterer, the right florist and goodness knows, the right whoever else. I nearly gave it all up and fled back to Hadleighwoode.

The hairdresser was but the first fiasco. He ran his fingers through my most luxuriant mane, felt its texture and threw up his hands. No amount of coaxing on the part of Aunt Kate, or guineas on the part of Nick could make him change his mind. He must look to his reputation and not present himself as a laughingstock to the *ton*.

Aunt Kate finally achieved the best hair style for me. She had her seamstress contrive a small pouch out of gauze the color of my dress and all of my hair was put into this and then the attached matching ribbons were tied around my head. Twice, we decorated the ribbons with flowers and I thought it was a comely addition but my opinion was my own and not generally accepted.

After my foot and hand measurements were taken, the haberdasher threw up his hands in disgust saying that never in his long and industrious career, had he been asked to produce shoes and gloves of such a size, at least not for a lady. Aunt Kate had learned, by this time, that firmness and an additional amount of guineas would produce almost anything one wished for and merely told him that if he could not, or would not, produce the desired articles, then we would simply take our business elsewhere.

He did not do it willingly, it is true but he finally agreed to at least try. And to everyone's surprise and pleasure, he did indeed produce acceptable slippers, gloves and the most wonderfully comfortable pair of demi-boots, the very thing for walking or riding. I was so pleased that I immediately ordered more pairs in every color that he could produce. We became quite good friends after all.

The seamstress was yet another débâcle. But in truth, it was not all her fault. The styles of the time were not meant for a female of my inches, being primarily the empire look that had come over from France. A one-piece garment, with a low neckline and little puffed sleeves, the very slightly full skirt was caught up just under the bosom and decorated with flowers or ribbons which were allowed to hang down toward the floor. Little narrow ribbons. Around the bottom of this dress, if it were a very fashionable garment, were several flounces or tiers of flounces, sometimes proceeding upward as far as the knees.

Indeed, it is a beautiful style but not for me. Whoever heard of flounces around the bottom of a young tree? That is exactly what I looked like. And, of course, those little narrow ribbons looked perfectly ridiculous on me The top portion of this fashion with its open neckline was very becoming to me but from that point downward, it was just disaster. I suggested that the ribbons be of a wider variety, or dispensed with altogether, which only prompted the seamstress to a fit of the vapors. I finally did succeed in convincing her to discard all but one flounce around the hemline.

When the gowns were delivered — and the sumptuousness of the fabrics quite overwhelmed me — I simply removed the ribbons myself and replaced them with wider ribbons or larger flowers. More to the proper size, shall we say? Of course, the colors were the usual insipid pastels, which are the required uniform of maidens and about which I could do nothing.

* * * * *

Then came the day, after nearly two months of preparations, when Joan and Aunt Kate finally deemed me ready to make my first venture into society and I was in alt! At last I should be in the position of every other young girl of good family and embark on my own delicious round of balls, routs, drums and Venetian breakfasts and other assorted fêtes! I was ready to take the *ton* by storm.

Our first outing certainly seemed harmless enough at the outset. Nick and Joan were patrons and thus held their own box at the Opera. Aunt Kate and I were to attend an opera with them. This seemed perfectly marvelous to me as I dearly love music but had never before heard an opera. I did not hear one that night either but it was not my fault that there was a near riot. Or at least I do not think it was. To begin with, I was totally unprepared for the general noise level and was also completely shocked by the absolute lack of attention that nearly everyone paid to what was happening on the stage. If they didn't want to observe what was happening on the stage, why did they come to the Opera House? Even Joan had no answers for my questions.

The brilliance of the candles for the stage was surpassed entirely by the grandeur presented by the audience. Every lady present was bedecked by jewels — in their hair, their ears, around their throats and wrists, or on the bodice of their gowns. The exhibition of the Crown Jewels at the Tower was trifling in comparison. The gentlemen were not left out of this display, either. Cravats were held in place by pins which were barely able to support the weight of the diamonds, rubies, emeralds or sapphires throwing sparks of fire in all directions and cuffs were sparkling and glittering with yet even more gems.

It was marvelous to be wearing my first real evening gown, made of a glorious light yellow silk, with the strand of pearls given to me by Nick snug around my throat. I felt truly grown up for the first time in my life. Nick's carriage, with his crest on the doors, was luxurious, Joan was inclined to be condescending under the weight and majesty of the Woode rubies and my head was in a whirl. Joan had promised to present me to any of the patronesses of Almack's who might be in attendance that night at the Opera and I was determined to be gracious and dignified so that I might be accepted into this society. How else was I to meet and marry in order to fulfill my dreams?

My spirits were temporarily quite deflated when I discovered that neither the Prince Regent nor Lord Wellington nor any of the Lady Patronesses or even William Lamb, the unfortunate husband of the notorious Caro, who'd made such a cake of herself over Lord Byron, had cared to grace us with their presence. However, Joan nodded and smiled to the inhabitants of most of the other boxes. I couldn't help but notice that she gave a special smile to a blond man across the way, inclining her head toward me as she did so. I puzzled over her actions for several moments but then the orchestra began to play and I aimed my wandering wits in the direction of the stage.

The opera was one composed by Mr. Haydn and I had never before heard of it, although I spent hours playing his compositions for the pianoforte. There were no well-known artists in this performance, Madame Catalini having had to withdraw at the last moment, because of a soreness in her throat. This apparently did not set well with the dandies in the pit who launched such a clamoring that it was impossible to hear anything. The orange-girls were set upon and all their oranges taken from them and then the oranges became projectiles directed at everyone and anyone close to the stage including a few unfortunates whose boxes were apparently too close to the front of the theater. Those ruffians who were not able to gather an orange for throwing seemed to have come prepared with other varieties of fruits and vegetables, suitable to their nefarious purposes.

After a few minutes this activity began to lose its enjoyment and the dandies stood down there on the floor, raised their quizzing glasses and proceeded to inspect carefully the inhabitants of each box. They appeared to find the area of our box the most interesting for this contemplation. In my innocence and wanting to know what they found so interesting, I stood up to better see what was happening.

Joan, who was sitting behind me, reached for my skirt to urge me back into my chair, tugged too hard and loosened the skirt where I had made the very slightest alteration to the original design by replacing the narrow little deep gold velvet ribbons with wider ones of the same color and texture. As the folds of material came toward her in her hand, I turned around to see what she wanted of me, which, of course, loosened even more of my apparently fragile handiwork. At the sight of my petticoat being available for anyone to see, she did the only thing a countess in that position could do. She swooned.

Nick jumped up to attend to her just as I was turning around and we bumped heads. He swore and as I moved away from him, I bumped into the railing around the box and I nearly toppled right over the edge! Aunt Kate grabbed my hand—she is ever-so much more practical—and pulled me back into my chair. By this time they could have been setting cannons off on the stage and no one could have heard them for the laughter and general hooting going on down in the pit.

As I looked around the boxes I could only see modish heads of hair fronted by fans placed carefully just so, in order that sparkling eyes could peep over them, or else gentlemen concealing their mouths. These elegant and bejeweled people did not want to be seen to be looking in the direction of our box but they were all apparently compelled to, just the same. I put my head down and started to weep for embarrassment but Aunt Kate swatted my arm with her fan and hissed, "Hold your head up and keep the tears for later." I looked at her in surprise and she whispered behind her fan, "If you don't hold your head up now, you'll never be able to hold it up again."

And so I held my head high, tears glittering but not falling and pasted a sickly smile on my lips. Nick was helping Joan to sit up in her chair and fanning her with her fan. Feverishly he looked around and found his evening cape which he handed to Aunt Kate and told her to somehow mend my garment and cover me with his cape. He would send for the carriage and we must be ready to leave in five minutes. He would instruct the footman to assist Joan.

We managed to leave the box and dispose ourselves in the carriage without further serious mishap, although as I was hurried out of the Opera House with my head down to hide my tears, I was nearly bowled over by a very large blond man who was very elegantly dressed in dark gold velvet and who appeared to be proceeding in the direction of our now vacated box.

I turned to get a better glimpse of him but my tears had blurred my vision somewhat and in the darkened corridor I nearly stumbled over the excess material of my skirt that had come loose from my grasp. He leaned toward me and clutched my arm, steadying me and for some reason I came out in gooseflesh. My arm tingled in the funniest way where his hand was touching me and I shivered at the intensity in his eyes as he looked down at me. I was grateful that the candles in their holders were not lit, so that no one else could see the tears silently flowing down my face.

"Bertie!" Aunt Kate's voice startled me from my bemusement and I pulled away from him, gathered up my skirts and rushed to join Aunt Kate. Even without Joan's harangue when we arrived back at Hadleigh House, I shall never forget that night.

Joan swished about her elegant drawing room like a tigress, saying she had never been so mortified, never! "How will I ever dare to show my face in society again?" And so forth. At first I was angry. How could it have been my fault that Madame Catalini had not sung, thus starting the near riot? But as Joan became more vehement in her complaints, I began to feel that perhaps I had been in some way responsible.

Tearfully I informed Nick that I wished to go home to Hadleighwoode and forget all about society if this was how it was conducted. And then to my amazement, Joan whirled on me. "No, madam, you will not", she screeched. "If I must hold my head up to quell this little fiasco, then you must hold your head up as well!" I was never so surprised.

She turned on Aunt Kate. "Next time before you take her out in public, you must inspect her very carefully to make sure she will not fall apart." *Swish.* "And you will have to, in some way, instill some manners in her." *Stalk.* To me, "Did no one ever tell you that a lady is never inquisitive?" *Pounce.* To Nick, "Why did I ever let you talk me into this?"

Finally, Joan wore down and collapsed onto the sofa. She glared at Aunt Kate, then at me and said, "You will both be here tomorrow morning at eleven. We must plan how we may salvage something of this. We might just pretend it didn't happen. I am quite sure that I have enough countenance to get by and," here she gritted her teeth, "my position as a society hostess will not suffer because of one green, er, girl. Is that clear?" She glared at each of us in turn. We all agreed. My stomach had never been so far from its normal place. It was absolutely under my feet. At the same time there was such a huge lump in my throat that I could barely swallow.

I longed for Hadleighwoode and Bessie. Once again I had been made, or had made of myself, a prime laughingstock and the protection of Joan's position as a hostess was all anyone could think of.

Aunt Kate and I were sent home in Nick's carriage and on our arrival there, she accompanied me to my room. Her maid Jane brought us cups of hot chocolate while Aunt Kate helped me out of my beautiful but now tattered gown and into my night rail. After I climbed into my warmed bed she stayed with me, sitting in a chair beside me holding my hand. She talked of our plans and preparations and how much she loved me until I went to sleep.

The moonlight coming through my window woke me when the house was all dark and quiet and I lay there thinking over the events of the past few weeks and what I had hoped for during the next months and years. I decided that I would make every effort to please Joan so that I might stay with Aunt Kate and Aunt Hattie for a bit longer in the hopes that Nick might find my husband for me. If that didn't transpire, then I should simply go back home to Hadleighwoode and learn how to be the best spinster aunt in the world! I rolled over, put the pillow over my head and fell into a deep slumber.

Chapter Four

London

⚏

At precisely eleven of the clock the next morning, Aunt Kate and I were allowed through the front door of Hadleigh House by Bunford, Joan's elegant and very starchy but Friday-faced butler. I thought I detected a faint sneer, or possibly it was a smirk on his usually impassive face but nevertheless he was all politeness.

After first handing Aunt Kate's and then my pelisse to a footman — Bunford would not soil his hands on such mundane duties — he said, "Madame awaits you in her room." At the snap of his white-gloved fingers — and I wondered once again how he does that — another footman, resplendent in the Woode livery of forest green and cream, appeared from seemingly nowhere to escort us up the winding stairway to Joan's room.

She greeted me with a curt nod and gave a tired smile to Aunt Kate. "At least you are prompt," she whispered. I flashed her a weak smile and gave myself up to a serious study of her room. It was the definition of opulent, with luxurious bed and window hangings of ivory brocade. The exquisite carpet was of the same shade. There were several tall windows behind the draperies and between each pair of windows was a golden sconce holding five candles. The furnishings were also of the same ivory color, giving one the feeling of having entered a colorless world. Joan, herself, provided the only relief in her frilly pink satin and lace negligee. I was truly stunned, having never seen so much elegant beauty in one place. I decided that when I was married and had charge of my own home, I too, should have just such a boudoir. Although perhaps with a bit of color here and there.

"Bertie!" I came to myself, jolted from my reverie. Joan was speaking to me. "It is truly regrettable that you made such a cake of yourself last evening, my girl. If it were not for my position and Nick's too of course, I should be most happy to send you back to the Dower House. But for his sake," she sighed, "I have decided to sponsor you myself with a small dinner here at Hadleigh House." She paused and looked at me. I wondered if I should get down on my knees to thank her—or perhaps I should lick her hand like a puppy seeking forgiveness for its mistakes. I did nothing because I did not know what to do. And I was wrong, again.

"Have you no sense of gratitude, girl?" Joan's voice was finding its strength.

"Oh yes, Joan," I said with what I hoped was a pleased smile. "I should like that above all things. It should be much easier to be introduced to society at a small dinner party in your lovely home." I looked to Aunt Kate for confirmation that I had said the right thing. She visibly relaxed and patted my hand.

Joan looked at me. "Ring for Bunford and tell him to send Hackett to me and then go and amuse yourself in the small drawing room." Hackett was Joan's woman of all work, laboring under the guise of secretary.

Bunford did his magical appearing act once more and I said, in my most imperious manner, "Send Hackett to my aunt, Bunford. I am to wait in the small drawing room." I succeeded in momentarily discomposing him by issuing two commands at one time. Naturally, I should not be allowed to find my own way to the small drawing room by myself but Madame could not be allowed to wait for Hackett either.

He nodded and said, "Please to wait here for just a moment, milady and I will have someone escort you." He backed away from me as if afraid to let me out of his sight—

what had he heard about me already? I had, after all, just arrived here in town. Looking around the foyer I could not see any dangers to me, or any potential for damage to be done by me. Anxious to stay on the good side of Joan however, I pretended I was a statue, hardly daring to breathe, until Bunford returned for the long journey to the second door down the hallway.

The small drawing room at the back of Hadleigh House was Joan's concession to the craze for all things oriental that was sweeping the country now that our Prince Regent had endorsed the style with his Pavilion at Brighton. The small drawing room at Hadleigh House could more properly have been called a Music Room as it contained, in addition to the Broadwood pianoforte, a harp glittering goldenly over in one corner and, in the opposite corner, a little harpsichord under a large fringed shawl.

The chairs were all lacquered with a black shiny finish and had bright red satin covers. There were golden dragons embroidered on the seats and backs, matching the dragons that were worked into the wall coverings. A large, mostly red patterned carpet covered the middle of the floor, matching with its flowers and trees—I learned later not trees but bamboo—the designs woven around the dragons on the walls. Not a particularly peaceful room but with a beauty not to be denied. Bunford drew back the draperies, exposing a view of the gardens.

I started toward the Broadwood and halted in the middle of the floor, looking around more carefully. No wonder Joan sent me in here. There were no small trinkets of the sort she so greatly admired. No little statuettes of the finest porcelain. In other words, nothing readily breakable. Heaving a huge sigh of relief, I continued to the Broadwood and sat down.

It was easy to lose myself in the music. Jon had always sent me sheets of piano compositions by Messrs. Beethoven, Mozart and Haydn and I prided myself on my good memory. I could play for hours without needing the music to be set in front of me but this time, after what seemed like only minutes, I heard a noise behind me and turned around.

Bunford was standing just inside the room with a maid and a footman just behind him. "Madame has ordered refreshment for you, milady. You may have it in here," this with a pained look on his face, "or", brightening a little, "in the morning room, as you prefer." I was not insensitive to his dismay at the thought of my contaminating this lovely room with crumbs and spills and so I stood up and walked over to the little group.

"Thank you, Bunford," I said. "I had not realized that it was so late. I think the morning room would do very nicely." And so our little caravan proceeded down the hallway to the third doorway on the right and into the morning room, so named because the morning sun billowed in through the nearly transparent coverings over the windows. The decorating was done in shades of yellow, from the palest cream to a rich buttercup hue. I loved the room and was most comfortable in it.

My nuncheon was set out and Bunford and his minions left me. I discovered that I was starving. After all, it takes a certain amount of food to keep one of my size in a happy condition. I was amazed that Bunford seemed to realize this, because the serving he had brought me was a very hearty one, really enough for two or three people. As I was ruminating on this fact, along with the food, the door burst open and in rushed a handsome gentleman of about the same age as Jon.

"I say, Nick—" He stopped and looked at me in total confusion. "I say, you aren't Nick. My apologies, ma'am."

Of course I had a muffin in my mouth and so I could only look at him helplessly.

"I do beg your pardon. Lord Turney, Robert Turney at your service." He bowed to me and I was quite impressed.

I swallowed the last of the muffin and smiled at him. "How nice to meet you, sir. I am Lady Zenobia Hadleigh, a sister of Nick, I should say, Lord Woode. I don't think he is at home at the present. Would you care to join me in my nuncheon?"

"Zenobia!" came a screech from the doorway. Now what had I done?

Joan, now dressed, rushed into the room. She simpered at Lord Turney. "This is my sister-in-law, Zenobia, my lord. Allow me to introduce you properly. Zenobia is just up from Hadleighwoode and is to make her debut this Season. Please forgive her lack of decorum as we have not yet had time to teach her all the ways of society. She will still imagine she is in the country." This rush of words directed at Lord Turney and with a smile for him, became a grimace in the fleeting look she gave to me.

Lord Turney was completely up to every rig and row in town, easily able to be condescending to Joan and conciliatory to me, all at the same time. A pleasant easy smile possessed his face. "Have sisters of my own, countess, no need to fret. "He turned the smile to me. "It is not really so awful, learning town manners, y'know," he assured me, winking at me with one large blue eye, carefully turned away from Joan. "It gets easier as you go on."

During all of this conversation, I had remained seated. I now stood up, catching Joan off guard and I watched Lord Turney's large blue eyes follow me. A range of expressions did battle for residency on his handsome face and I nearly laughed out loud. Instead I coughed. He gained control of his features and stammered, "Yes...ah, how nice to have met you, Lady...ah...Zenobia." He turned to Joan, extended his hand and made an elegant leg. "Countess. I must have misunderstood Nick, er, Lord Woode. I'll take my leave, then and look for him elsewhere."

Joan placed her dainty hand in his and I watched enviously as he raised it to his lips. She inclined her head slightly and with a somewhat pensive smile, Lord Turney left the room.

I sat back down and hung my head. I expected Joan to ring a peal over me, so I thought I might as well make it easier for her. Instead there was silence. Preparing to move swiftly out of the way if necessary, I raised my head to look at her and discovered, to my surprise, that she had seated herself and was now calmly staring at me, a more or less neutral expression on her face. Surprise rendered me speechless.

She looked intently at me for a moment, then said in a calm voice, totally unlike the voice she usually used when speaking to me, "Strange to say, you don't particularly look like a ninny. I wonder why it is that you always contrive to act like one. I have heard Jon tell Nick how quickly you learned from his school books. Indeed, they quite feared you might turn into a bluestocking. And you are certainly more than passable on the pianoforte." My face turned scarlet with pleasure at her offhand compliment. She continued, "I do not know how we shall go on if you will not at least make an attempt to learn the ways of society."

Calmly she sat there, drumming her fingers on the table.

"Joan, I am truly sorry that I have distressed you. I would not have done it for the world. And indeed I don't know what I have done that is so wrong. Should I not have invited Lord Turney to share my nuncheon? There seemed so much more than I could eat—"

She interrupted me. "There is nothing at all wrong with offering to share your nuncheon—"

I heaved a huge sigh of relief.

"Except", she went on, raising her fingers and tugging at the first one, "no young lady may remain in a room alone with a young man unless that young man is a relative. Under no circumstances. Marriages have been done for less." The second finger received its turn. "And, never would you say one word you could not help to a young gentleman to whom you have not been properly introduced." She turned to me with a puzzled look. "You haven't, you've never—?"

"Oh no, ma'am, I'd never met him before. I don't think I've ever even seen him before today," I assured her, smiling. This much at least I did know.

"Well there you are, then. Introductions are everything. Remember that. You must be properly introduced to any young gentleman before you may speak. Concerning young ladies, the rules are somewhat less restrictive. You may introduce yourself to a young lady of quality and converse with her, as long as the situation itself is unexceptionable. For instance, if you meet at a party, or a fashionable shop, or even in the park." She stopped for a moment and I could see on her face that she was mentally recounting all those sorts of places that I might ever be. "But not, of course, on the street. You should not be alone on the streets, ever, anyway, so that situation shouldn't arise."

This seemed an easy rule to remember so I smiled at her. "I think I should have no difficulty in following that instruction, Joan but please tell me what should I have done when Lord Turney burst in on me?"

"What—? My dear, had you no servants at Hadleighwoode before I came there? You should have rung for Bunford, who would have known how to extricate you from such a perilous situation. I do not precisely wish you to consult Bunford as an arbiter, you will understand but I can assure you that Bunford knows more about these things than even I do. When you set up housekeeping on your own, you could not do better for yourself and your husband, of course, than to engage a superior butler such as Bunford."

"Ah marriage," I said. The all-important subject. "Joan, do you think I shall ever marry?"

"What a bufflehead you are! What else should you do? Do you not know that Nick and I are taking steps to ensure it?"

"I don't think I quite understand what you mean by taking steps, Joan," I said.

"Nick is investigating those families of the proper rank who have sons of a marriageable age and who can afford the proper settlement. When we have found someone suitable we shall then tell you all about him and arrange a meeting. I think St. George's will be the perfect place for your wedding, as it was for ours."

I was too stunned to speak. She was lost again, in reminiscing about her wedding. In truth, it had been lovely and had made a big impression on us, yet I couldn't help but feel that I was missing out on a few of the important steps between now and the time of my own wedding.

I found my voice, more or less and said, "But, Joan, what if we shouldn't suit? What if I don't love — ?"

"Love?" Now it was her turn to be stunned. "Whatever has love to do with anything?" Joan was truly startled by my rash statement. "No one marries for love, my dear but in most cases, you will feel affection for each other and Nick will take care to have it understood that once you have filled your nursery, you will not then have to be in each other's pockets all of the time."

Again my face turned scarlet. "About filling the nursery, Joan. I didn't, don't, really understand — Bessie tried to explain matters once but I — "

"Well I should certainly hope not!" she exclaimed. "We have not even found you a suitable husband yet. There is plenty of time to talk about nurseries. Don't even think about such things yet. It isn't seemly."

"But, how will I know — ?"

Through her clenched teeth, she said, "Not another word, Zenobia. Do you understand that? Not an-oth-er word."

Rising from the chair with her usual grace, she left the room, shaking her head. I put my head on my arms and let the tears flow.

"Harrumph," said a voice in a low tone. I raised my head, to see who or what it was.

"Excuse me, Lady Zenobia but is there anything I might do for you?" Bunford was standing the correct three feet from my elbow, looking at my tearstained face with a mixture of disgust and concern on his face. I wondered what had happened to his starch. I was so unused to being called Lady that I had to stop myself from looking around to see whomever it was that he was addressing in such a manner. At home, in Hadleighwoode, I was just Bertie or miss. I missed that familiarity.

"No, thank you, Bunford." I discovered an untouched muffin and absently started to put butter on it. "I think I don't like society very much. It isn't at all what I had expected. I wish I could go home to Hadleighwoode."

"Oh no, milady. Once you become familiar with the established patterns, so to speak, you'll be happy and like it above all things." He was so serious and I wanted so much to believe him. "Perhaps, milady, you might like to go for a walk. If I might suggest the Park? I could summon one of the maids to accompany you."

I looked out the window at the sun-bathed garden and found a small smile for him. "Yes, Bunford. I should like that. Please do. I'll just run up and get my bonnet."

As I was rushing to gather my bonnet, pelisse and gloves I chanced to catch a glimpse of myself in the mirror. Horrors! No wonder Bunford was more Friday-faced than usual. Hurriedly I dashed some cool water on my tearstained cheeks and dragged a brush over the front of my hair. I wished to do more but was afraid that Bunford might change his mind, so I gathered my belongings and went flying down the stairs.

A frightened-looking young maid jumped out of my way. Bunford looked at me. His face had found its starch again, along with a good helping of ice. "Lady Zenobia, this is Millie," he said, motioning to the young girl to step forward once again. "She is to accompany you everywhere once you leave this house." He looked at Millie, who seemed to shrink visibly at his words. "Do you understand that, Millie? You must not let Lady Zenobia out of your sight." He looked at me again. I flinched under that glare.

"It is Millie's purpose, Lady Zenobia, to see that you do not get lost, or come to any harm. I trust that you will accept the responsibility for her, as she does for you." He took the pelisse from my shaking hands and waited for me to put on the bonnet. As he held the pelisse high enough to slip over my shoulders, he added, "If you think you might wish to do any shopping, milady, then you should also have a footman to accompany you. Shall I send for one, Lady Zenobia?"

"No, thank you, Bunford. I can't think of anything that I might need. I seem to have too much of everything as it is." I reached for Millie's hand, which after a first tentative reach in my direction, scuttled back into her sleeve, accompanied by a frosty look from Bunford.

"Millie knows her place my lady. We will not send a footman today then," and he turned away to open the front door. "Please remember that the countess wishes to have tea at four, so be sure to return by then."

With those words of admonishment, he bustled us out the door and closed it quietly behind us. We went down the five steps in silence. I looked down at Millie and smiled at her. She did not smile back. "Oh Millie, please. This is the first time I've been allowed out without Joan or Aunt Kate to lead me around. It is such a lovely day I cannot bear to not smile. It would please me if you could smile too." I suddenly realized that I had not heard her say one word yet. What if she was incapable of speech?" Do you know where Hatchard's Book Shop is and Gunther's?" I asked.

Her mouth opened and her lips moved but it was such a timid little squeak that I could not understand her. I moved closer to hear her better but she backed up even farther away from me. "Millie," I began.

"Oh please milady, I must stay behind you and I cannot go farther back the railing is in my way. Please step back." I was so startled at this speech that I did indeed step back onto the walkway.

"What do you mean that you must stay behind me?" I asked. "However should we talk if you are behind me?"

"Please milady we do not talk. I am only to accompany you as you walk so that you will not be alone. Should we not go now — please, milady?" She looked up at me with a look I could not fathom. It seemed to be equal parts of fear and confusion. I wondered if she thought my name was "please milady"?

"Millie, my name is —" Her eyes became even larger and she pulled away from me once again.

"Oh no milady, I couldn't. It would mean my place, milady." Her little chin became firmer as she said this. Now I was confused.

She took a deep breath and speaking firmly and clearly, said, "Milady this is not your village, this is London and I don't know who made what rules or why. I only know that no young lady talks to her maid on the street and no young lady may be friends with her maid and if you do not wish to walk milady, then please do say so and we can go back inside and I can get back to my work. Please milady, I do need this position as it's the best one I've ever had." She ran out of words and breath at the same time and just looked at me imploringly.

I was trying to work out the ramifications of her words, when she repeated, "Please, milady?"

"Do you mean that we may not go to Gunther's for an ice after we walk, if you may not speak to me?" At last I saw a spark of anticipation on her face.

"Milady, Hatchard's and Gunther's are near each other, or near enough that if we find one, we should certainly be able to find the other. Or is it perhaps Hookham's that you mean? They both have lending libraries. We simply walk until you need to turn your direction and I call out, 'right', or 'left, milady', as need be. I don't know about Gunther's, milady. I've never been there."

"Millie I cannot imagine a walk such as you describe, but I am eager enough to stretch my le—er, have some fresh air, that I am willing to at least try. Perhaps when we reach Gunther's we shall be able to observe how other young ladies and their maids go on."

And so we set out on my first walk in London. Although I couldn't see what we looked like in actuality, I immediately remembered a goose and her goslings walking around the lake at Hadleighwoode and felt sure that we must resemble them in very truth.

It was not a very pleasant walk as I knew that I dared not really stride out as I was used to do at home lest I lose Millie in the crowds. I wanted to look about me and see the houses and the people that we were passing but there was not enough time to inspect our surroundings and still have time to browse through the book shop. The only good thing was that it was not raining. I had thought that if it should be at all wet the walkways would have been mud higher than my ankles. However the walkways were neatly cobbled and thus exceptionally clean and neat.

The fresh warm air felt very pleasant but I determined that the next time I was allowed out I would go in a carriage or barouche. Nick had several conveyances in his stables as well as a multitude of horses.

Lost in my thoughts, I suddenly felt a tug on my right arm. I whirled around, only to find a frustrated-looking Millie at my elbow. "Please, milady," she whispered, "turn to your right, here, milady." I looked up to discover that we were indeed at a corner. She looked as though tears were not far from the surface of her eyes. "I did say 'right, milady' three times. I'm sorry I touched your arm but you wouldn't hear me."

"Millie there is so much noise out here that I am afraid you will have to shout if I am to hear you since you insist on remaining behind me," I answered her. "Surely, we are far enough away from Mayfair that you could walk beside me," I started to say but at the look on her face, stopped and said, "Oh very well let us continue. To the right here you say?"

She nodded and we went to the right. After a few more turns we were suddenly in an area where the walking was much easier underfoot and where there were even more people, not to mention carriages, barouches, landaulets and young men on horseback. The entire front of this square seemed to be windows full of merchandise and the third one we passed did indeed have books. I turned to Millie, "Are you to come in with me?"

"Oh no, milady, I will wait for you here," she said.

"You mean to let me out of your sight, then?" I asked.

A look of sheer terror passed over her face. "Oh milady, I—watch out!" she screamed. I had backed up to get a better look at the sign over the door and inadvertently stepping backward into the street had come perilously close to being run down by a young dandy riding his horse much too fast for such a busy place. Millie's voice took on a more commanding tone. "Milady, if it means my place I cannot leave you alone for one minute, I think. Come, we will go in together."

We went into the bookstore and I came to an immediate halt, causing Millie to run into the back of me. Never had I seen so many books in one place before and I was too entranced to move. When another patron ran into the back of Millie I was forced to take a few more steps into the room and then I just stood there gazing about at the shelves of books and music.

There were tables with chairs around them scattered throughout the room, some of them occupied by both ladies and gentlemen, busily perusing the books and not conversing with each other. The silence reminded me of a church and indeed the feeling of being in a hallowed place kept me quiet.

After a few moments of looking around I headed for a shelf across the room, labeled "History". There was no one else looking at these books, although I noticed a cluster of ladies in front of the shelves labeled "Fiction". Romances, I presumed. Taking down a book I used it to cover my still fascinated gazing around the room. I noticed a section devoted to music and started in that direction.

I must admit that I was so bemused I was not watching where I was going, so I immediately ran into a wall and dropped the book I was carrying. As I bent down to pick it up I noticed that the wall had feet! Hurriedly I straightened up to apologize for my preoccupation and raising my eyes to their ordinary level I found myself looking at a mouth. This had hardly ever happened to me before and my own jaw dropped in astonishment!

The mouth and it was indeed a very well-favored one, smiled. Hesitantly I looked upward and discovered the most handsome face I had ever seen. Green eyes sparkling with amusement were the most commanding feature, followed closely by that smile and a mop of golden curls in glorious, but carefully contrived disarray, which surmounted the whole. The giant said nothing, just stood there and smiled at me. I could not see anything at all humorous in the situation and took refuge in my confusion.

I felt a faint nudge of familiarity but couldn't quite place him. Perhaps it would come to me later. He was positively huge in his multi-caped greatcoat and I was entranced, in spite of myself.

I tried to apologize but could not seem to find my voice. I looked down at his expensively booted feet, then up at his face again. I swallowed hard. A soft rumble broke the silence as he said, "Do I meet with your approval, then, Lady Bertie?"

I was so surprised at hearing my family's name for me emerge from his mouth that I dropped my book again. I began to lean down to pick it up when he clasped my hand in one of his great paws. I gasped from the shock and the fact that my arm tingled under his touch. Never before had I experienced anything like this. I longed to speak to him, ask him his name and how he knew my name but Joan's very positive and very recent strictures stuck in my mind, rendering me speechless. Meanwhile, Millie rushed to pick up the books and then tugged at my elbow.

"Please milady, if you are to be home in time for tea with Her Ladyship I think we should leave now." He released my arm and bowed slightly. I took my book to the counter and signed for it. Millie immediately took charge of it and motioned to the door with her head. My mind was preoccupied with thoughts of him. He truly did seem vaguely familiar in a way I could not quite understand and in the hope of jostling my memory I couldn't resist taking one last look over my shoulder. Immediately I wished I hadn't, because he was still standing there head held high, almost arrogantly, smiling at me. Before I could turn my head around again to pay attention to where I was going I had bumped into a lady on her way into the store.

A laugh which sounded like friendly thunder rolled across the room, as the newcomer pulled herself together and said, "Well really!'" I could not hear the rest of what she was saying as Millie took my arm and rushed me through the doorway.

When we were once again out-of-doors, I took a deep breath to steady myself. "Millie do you have any idea who that gentlemen could be? And how could he have known my name? I know I have never been introduced to him for I would surely remember that!" Indeed, I should remember him for all of my life!

"No milady. How would I know such a thing?"

"Of course." I sighed. "Do you know which way to Gunther's? I should enjoy an ice, wouldn't you?"

She frowned and said in her sad little voice, "I don't think we have time, milady. It would be best to go back now. Do you remember the way?"

"Would it really be so terrible if I were a few minutes late for tea?"

"Please milady, I would be in trouble."

"I could explain—"

"No milady, not today. Please?"

"Do you think you might ever say, 'Lady Bertie'?" I asked.

"Please, Lady Bertie," she said, saying each syllable slowly and clearly. "Could we please return now? You will be late for tea and I will lose my position."

Faced with such determination, I turned and began the trudge homeward to Mayfair and Hadleigh House. Except for those few moments in the bookstore this entire experience had been a sad disappointment, just as had everything else I had done in London. How do such high expectations end up in such perfectly awful realities?

And how had that giant known my name? Was I already a subject of tattle for the *ton*, when I had not yet even made my come-out? I felt I should explode with questions but at the same time, knew that Joan must not know anything about this latest escapade for fear that she would indeed ring a peal over me. But if I could not ask anyone anything about him, how should I ever find out who he was?

I wondered idly if he might perhaps be a connection of Sean's, visiting from Ireland. Those green eyes were certainly a Brett family characteristic, as was the golden hair and the sheer size of the man. Certainly he had mentioned a brother, had he not? I tried to imagine this man with longer hair and a beard and found myself unable to do so in my mind. Mayhap pen and paper would enable me to produce a recognizable sketch and I could ask Tyler about him. Another niggle wandered through the empty space of my mind. My memory was a bit hazy but I did think this man was not quite as large as I remembered Sean to be. Ah, well.

Patience is not my strong suit, even though I once overheard someone say I was as placid as a cow chewing her cud. I did wonder what prompted the laughter in these situations but my appearance brought a halt to that particular conversation, so I never did learn. I concluded that they really did not mean me in that reference, because I never considered myself to be placid at all. My mind was still reeling with all these inanities mixed with a sprinkling of thoughts about the giant, when Millie tugged at my elbow and said with a distinct touch of relief, "We're here, milady."

Chapter Five

ഇ

Bunford was waiting for us. An unspoken signal seemed to pass between him and Millie. He reached for my pelisse, saying, "Did you enjoy your walk, Lady Bertie?"

"Oh yes Bunford. It was everything that was wonderful." My sarcasm eluded him. As I walked up the stairs to my room to prepare myself for tea I said under my breath, "I hope I may never have such a wonderful time again any time soon."

"Lady Bertie," Bunford called to my retreating back, "Where do you wish to have me place your books?"

In truth I could not answer him as I wished to, so I did not answer him at all. I knew I was being unreasonable and one should never take out one's anger on the servants unless they were the direct cause of the anger. Even then one must not rampage. But I felt that if I opened my mouth to say anything to him I could not be responsible for whatever I might utter.

I washed my face and brushed my hair. As I was tying the ribbon, I realized that I could not appear for tea in my walking dress and promptly burst into tears. In order to be a young lady of fashion it seemed necessary to change one's clothes at least six or even eight times a day. How much more sensible as at dear Hadleighwoode to simply get dressed in the morning for whatever one planned to do that day and then not to have to change again until time to don one's nightclothes. Why did I ever think I wanted to be a young lady of fashion? But here I was and I might as well make the most of it.

There was a knock at the door. I brushed the tears away and went to open it. Hackett stood there. "It is nearly time for tea and I thought you might wish some assistance in changing."

"Hackett that is quite the nicest thing anyone has said to me all day." I motioned for her to come into the room. "Will we be just family or do we have guests, do you know?" I asked.

"Well milady, I rather suspect that you might say both, I think."

"Both Hackett? How is this?"

"Your brother Lord Tyler, arrived this afternoon milady and so you do have a guest but he is family." She may have been planning to say more but I inadvertently stifled her with a giant hug.

"Oh Hackett, thank you. That is the very best of news! Is he alone? What is he doing? Does he —?"

"I suggest, my dear, that once you are dressed you might go downstairs and ask him these questions yourself. You will not want to keep the countess waiting you know."

"No. As usual you are quite correct. What do you think of this one?" I asked, holding up a blue muslin day dress. It was another one that I had renovated by myself and was very pleased with the results. It now had bows of the same colored ribbon fastened all around under the bosom and at the one flounce. I had a matching ribbon for my hair.

I flung the renovated garment at the bed and began to undo the buttons of my walking dress. Two of them resisted my efforts and flew across the room. Hackett went to retrieve them. "I'll just take this shall I and put the buttons back on?" she asked my back. I was already out of the door and on my way downstairs, tying my ribbon as I went.

"Tyler, Tyler, where are you?" I called.

Bunford crept up behind me and said, "I will be most happy to take you to Lord Tyler, milady." I dropped my ribbon. Showing remarkable restraint, Bunford picked it up and handed it to me without saying a word.

He preceded me down the hallway to the small drawing room and opened the door for me. I managed a sedate entrance I thought and strolled across the room to Tyler.

"And here is my favorite hoyden," that young man said with a smile.

"Hoyden? Me? Don't you mean Bessie?" I said as I was enveloped in his arms. "Oh Tyler, it is so very good to see you. Where have you been? What have you been doing?" I asked his shoulder. It was such a nice, comforting shoulder.

Disentangling himself, he led me to the sofa. "We'll just sit here and have a nice coze, shall we?" he asked. "You must tell me what you have been up to and how you managed to cause such a disruption at the opera last night. You are quite the subject of gossip today you know." He could not keep from laughing. "Joan is quite out of sorts with you."

"But it wasn't my fault Tyler, truly it wasn't. Madame Catalini did not sing, which started the fuss. Oranges and everything else it seemed, were flying through the air and I just wanted to see what was happening. If Joan hadn't grabbed my gown—well if I had perhaps put a few more stitches in it—oh anyway, it, my gown that is, came apart and my petticoat, ah and Joan swooned and I nearly fell over the railing—but Aunt Kate kept me in the box, though."

I stopped talking and looked at Tyler in indignation. He was laughing too hard to be listening. Or so it seemed to me. He pulled out his handkerchief and mopped his face. He looked at me and started laughing again. It was such an infectious laugh that I giggled too. Soon we were both laughing and crying with tears streaming down our faces. I tried to stand up to walk around the room for a bit to ease the ache in my side but found my legs too weak to support me and collapsed into a nearby chair. Then I hiccupped sending Tyler off again.

"Oh brat, you have not changed have you?" he cried. "You have always been able to make a perfectly simple occasion into a—um." He looked at my face and suddenly stopped.

"Tyler, it really wasn't my fault, although I know I shall take the blame for it. I don't like it here in London at all. I don't know why I ever thought I should. I wish only to go back to Hadleighwoode, to Bessie and the aunts. Please Tyler, can you help me to do this?"

"But you've not been here for two months yet and out only one time," he answered. "Just be patient. You'll come to love it here. Wait until you go to Almack's, or some of the parties and balls—"

"If last night is any sample, I shall not like it at all. And today too." Remembering the supposed walk that Millie and I had taken, I decided to ask Tyler if that was the way all young ladies were to behave. And what about that giant? Maybe Tyler would know about him. "Today Bunford suggested that I might like to take a walk. But this was after I had invited a Lord Turney to share my nuncheon—"

"You did what?" Tyler was suddenly listening intently. "Turney, here? And when were you presented to him?" His voice bristled.

"Well but you see, I hadn't been presented to him. He came into the morning room as I was having my nuncheon and there was so much of it, really enough for two or three persons, so I thought—"

"But what was he doing in the morning room? Where was Bunford? Does Turney have the run of the house?"

"I don't know where Bunford was, nor do I care. He has nothing to do with this. I do wish you would listen to what I am saying." I gave him my most forbidding look. "All I do know is that Lord Turney came in looking for Nick and he seemed like a nice young man and so I invited him—"

"Bertie, Turney's the very worst rake in town! If you ever expect to make a good match, you must not have anything more to do with him." I just stared at him. "Of course, they do say that a reformed rake makes the best husband." His voice died away. "No, I don't really think so, in your case."

"But Tyler, this was only nuncheon!"

"Oh Lord, brat. Even in your own morning room, er, I should say Joan's morning room, you can't keep away from trouble. Has no one explained things to you yet?"

"Yes, after I do the wrong thing I am positively encumbered with explanations of the right thing. It is not much help. Joan explained a multitude of things to me—" My voice died away as I remembered the rest of Joan's explanations. "Tyler, how does one set up one's nursery? Bessie once tried to explain that but I was sure she had been out in the sun too much—"

A strangled cry from Tyler brought me to a halt. He was pulling at his cravat and wiping his face with his handkerchief. His face was quite flushed. I jumped up from the chair and ran over to the window. "Are you ill, Tyler? Shall I open a window for some air? Tyler? Tyler?" He was laughing again, meanwhile pounding the arm of Joan's delicate sofa with his fist. I was flummoxed.

It was obvious to me that Tyler was incapable of talking. I could hear his labored breathing, with an occasional gasp. After several minutes of this, he calmed down a little. He looked at me and his lower lip started to quiver. "Never say that nuncheon and nurseries were part of the same invitation to Turney? No wonder Joan—"

"Tyler," I said, in my most stern voice. "Are you foxed? At this time of the day? What do nuncheon and nurseries have to do with each other? They don't—" I stopped. Did they? Could they? Oh no! I felt the color rise in my face.

Fortunately, just at this time, Bunford opened the door and Nick came in. He walked over to Tyler and gave me a quizzing look as he passed by me. "Tyler old man, good to see you," he said as he walked over to the tray of decanters on a small Oriental table. "Join me?" he asked. Tyler only nodded, as he was still incapable of coherent speech.

"I'll have one too, please Nick," I said, calmly.

As usual, Nick's benign demeanor invaded whatever room he was in and a very pleasant few minutes were spent in general conversation, although I noticed that Tyler would not or could not look at me. They did not discuss the previous evening, only some generalities of Hadleighwoode, or Nick's current concerns in the Lords. Whenever it looked as though I might open my mouth to contribute to the conversation, Tyler shook his head at me. He volunteered a few comments about his more genteel activities, mills and fights and such. I didn't pay much attention to these as I was still puzzling over nuncheons and nurseries and giants. I became aware of Nick saying my name.

"Bertie, Bertie! Did you hear what I was saying?" Nick asked. Numbly, I shook my head. "Joan has decided that we will, after all, go to Lady Colney's musicale this evening. If you would like to, that is." He looked at me, with that loving smile. *Oh Nick*, I thought, *if only there could be, somewhere, another such as you.*

"If Joan thinks it to be advisable, then I will willingly go. What exactly is a musicale? I should like to be prepared."

Tyler muttered under his breath, although I heard him quite easily. "Forewarned, you mean."

"It is just a small, private sort of concert, a few performers only, such as yourself, perhaps."

"Me?" I shrieked.

"No, no, not this time. I meant only that persons of the quality, like ourselves, sometimes a singer or two, or a string trio or quartet, or a soloist on the pianoforte will perform and then at the conclusion some small refreshments, that sort of thing. Very unexceptionable."

"Very small refreshments," this from Tyler.

"Will there be dancing or any other form of entertainment?" I asked.

"There usually is not," Nick answered. "Joan has mentioned that we may have such an evening here in a week or two, probably in this room," he said as he looked at the pianoforte and the harp. "I'm sure that if she does she would wish you to play. You are quite good, you know."

Tyler stood up and adjusted his cravat. He looked at Nick but had still not looked at me. "Do you mean to go, then? I had an invitation as did Simon and Gareth. We had not really meant to go but if you do think to attend, mayhap I shall see if they wish to as well."

"Ah, the 'younglings' are back in action, are they?" Nick turned back to me. "It's up to you, puss," he said. I felt a flash of uneasiness at the thought of seeing Tyler's friends once again. Nick, unaware, continued, "Actually, that's why I came down here. Joan thought you might like it. She said you had not had a very happy day." Tyler made a funny noise. Nick and I both looked at him.

"Remind me to tell you some time," he said to Nick. He smiled at me finally. "I won't tell you to be good, because it won't take," he said to me. "A musicale, now, should be harmless, even for you! Yes, I think I shall go and as many of the other younglings as I can find." He came back to me and kissed me on the cheek. As he started back to the door again it opened and Bunford stood aside allowing Joan to enter. A footman, carrying the tea tray followed her and following him was Bunford to oversee and supervise the happening. The hall clock chimed four times.

Joan looked at Tyler. "We are just having tea, Tyler."

He took her hand in his, kissed it and smiled down at her. "Thank you m'dear but I must go find the younglings. We will join you later this evening at Lady Colney's."

"Oh are we to go then also?" she looked at Nick, then at me. I could almost believe she really meant it when she said,

"How nice." Bunford directed the footman to place the tea things on the table by Joan's chair and Tyler left the room.

It was a perfectly unexceptionable tea.

* * * * *

Perhaps thirty minutes later, Joan rang for Bunford. She turned to me and said "Kate should be ready to return to Hattie's by now. Nick and I will call for you in our carriage at nine of the clock and we shall all go together to Lady Colney's." She rose from her chair and smiled at me. "It will do you good to have a quiet evening out in society my dear. Mayhap the opera wasn't the best choice for your first appearance. A musicale is a much smaller and more modest occasion and should be enjoyable for you since you like music so much." We all reached the door just as Bunford opened it. How ever does he do that?

Aunt Kate, looking rather harried and disarranged as though she had been working as a drudge all day, was waiting for me in the foyer. We all said our goodbyes and went out to the carriage. Patting my hand and smiling at me, Aunt Kate said, "You've no idea how fortunate you are my girl, that Joan is still willing to lend you her countenance. Please do try to not disgrace her again. I have no idea how much countenance she really has. If she has as much as she thinks she does, we may yet come out of all this still in prime twig."

"Aunt Kate," I said, "I think that I have made a great mistake. Society and I shall never make a match. I never dreamed that there would be so many silly rules that are just incomprehensible to me. I have managed to reach the age of one and twenty and now am made to feel the silliest girl, as though I should still be kept in an under-nursery, if there were such a thing. Truly, I think I should go back home to Bessie and Hadleighwoode. Perhaps I shall model myself after you and live happily ever after, just being an aunt." I sighed with longing.

"You are all about in your wits, my girl. Of course, you cannot do such a thing. You will go on splendidly, if only you will remember to think before you do or say anything."

In all fairness, I could not dispute this statement. Residing in the peacefulness of Hadleighwoode, I was used to saying or doing as I wished. Of course, there could be no dreadful repercussions from such actions there. Is it any wonder why I loved Hadleighwoode!

The carriage stopped and Simpson, Aunt Hattie's butler, came out and lowered the steps for us. Once safely in the hall we gave up our pelisses and Aunt Hattie came to welcome us. Really! We'd been out of the house for about seven hours and it might as well have been seven days the way everyone carried on. Aunt Hattie was short and plump and tended to bustle around. She did so now. "Joan sent a note saying that we are all to go to the musicale this evening at the home of Lord and Lady Colney. I have taken the liberty of laying out appropriate clothing and have ordered baths for you both. First though, you must rest for a while, then we can have a light supper before you make yourselves ready. Now upstairs with both of you. Shoo.!" She actually said, "Shoo!"

Against my will I accepted a cup of hot chocolate from Aunt Hattie and lay down for a short rest. My head whirled with a mixture of the events of the day and thoughts of Hadleighwoode, accompanied by images of the giant—I still wished I knew his name. I was startled a few moments later to be wakened by Aunt Kate's Jane, come to make me ready for the evening's entertainment. I was amazed to discover that I had slept for two hours!

Everything progressed just as Aunt Hattie had planned and exactly as the clock chimed nine we heard the carriage arrive. We were ready. As I was standing there, waiting I kept feeling little tugs at the skirt of my gown and looked around to find both aunts pulling here and there. "Just checking, dear," they chorused. Of course they were. I should not fall apart so easily this night!

I was wearing a light green satin dress with an overskirt of a darker green gauze and large green satin roses around the hem. It looked quite pretty, I thought. My hair was bound in one of Aunt Kate's contraptions, with another of the large roses on one side of the back. Green is very becoming to me and I felt presentable enough even for Court.

Perhaps this feeling imbued me with some sort of inner confidence, because the evening was both very pleasant and, more importantly from my standpoint at least, uneventful. The musicians were not of a professional level, of course but not all that amateurish either. I should have felt right at home with them but as I was not invited I could not participate. No matter. The light refreshments consisted of a wine punch and some little biscuits interspersed with small cakes that were delicious.

Tyler was there with two of the younglings, Simon Anthony and Gareth Spencer, whom he brought over to present to me. I hadn't seen either of them since that long ago day at the Circus and a shiver of apprehension ran up my spine. I was sitting on a sofa at the time and when I started to stand up, Tyler motioned me to remain seated, so I did. Simon sat down on one side of me and Gareth on the other. Tyler pulled up a chair next to Simon and we enjoyed a cozy talk for quite some while. They were so easy in their conversation that I seemed to forget about past experiences as well as current society and truly enjoyed myself, just being me. It was wonderful.

The younglings had been an inseparable group of six, Tyler, Simon, Gareth, Harry, Anthony and Sean. We would not see Anthony again as he had fallen at Waterloo. Sean's whereabouts remained a mystery to me and, I fancied, to my brothers as well. Thus, there were still four very active marriageable men greatly in demand at all of the social events of the Season available to ease my path into society. And, of course, that of other young ladies as well. I didn't care to think about that aspect for very long.

I could, however, easily understand their great popularity as they were all obviously well-born, handsome and usually well mannered. Simon and Gareth were not quite as tall as Tyler but still close to six feet in height. It was not difficult to see why they would be looked upon by some mamas as presentable escorts and by papas as eligible husbands.

They would not, perhaps, inherit their family title but were assured of enough income to live well and their birth guaranteed them entrée into any level of society. Their days were filled with those activities common to young gentlemen of their rank—sparring or milling at Gentleman Jackson's, perfecting their shooting skills at Manton's and frequenting fashionable tailors such as Weston and Stutz and patronizing the inimitable Hoby for boots.

An occasional visit to Tattersall's to discuss the prime horseflesh available there—and even to make a purchase—or perhaps a session with a fencing master served to occupy the balance of their time and to establish their eminent eligibility. Evenings, of course, were spent in a constant round of parties, balls and other such functions. An evening bereft of such an activity would find them at one of the various gentlemen's clubs to which they belonged—White's or Boodles, or one of the many other exclusive establishments in St. James'.

Such is the life of the unmarried young man of fashion. Envy stirred in me at the unfairness of it all. I must occupy my time in being seen in the right places, in the right mode of dress, in the company of the right persons and if none of these opportunities presented themselves, then I must just stay at home and occupy myself as best I might.

I longed to discuss all of this with the younglings but knew that to do so would only make them uncomfortable. My head was still whirling with the events of the day and especially with the giant who had accosted me at Hookham's but he would just have to wait until I found a better opportunity to question Tyler about him.

When I remarked that I hoped to be returning to Hadleighwoode in a few weeks, I was given hasty assurances that they would be pleased to call on me while I was still in town and would once again be pleased to return to Hadleighwoode also. We should plan an outing, or perhaps a hunt.

Indeed, I enjoyed myself so much that I was truly sorry when the evening came to an end. How I wished that this had been my first evening out and that we had never thought of the opera. I hummed to myself all the way home.

* * * * *

From that evening, events seemed to settle into a round of evenings out and evenings in, always in pleasant company. None of the functions were of a large nature, that is no grand balls but they were all enjoyable and I began to feel that perhaps I could enjoy London. I should have known better.

Joan had her dinner party and, surprisingly, it was a success from my viewpoint. Although men outnumbered the ladies, other than the younglings, there were no other guests of my age. Having spent so much of my life in the company of older people, I found it no hardship to converse with the two Generals and their ladies, or the three members of the Lords who were also present. Every time I was tempted to add to the conversation, I pinched myself first and thus did not betray my naiveté. I did not try to dazzle them in any way, except when Joan asked me to perform for them on the pianoforte.

The younglings—three of them plus Tyler—hovered around me and I felt quite the young lady of fashion. The gown I was wearing on this evening was very becoming to me, being a light bluish green in color and trimmed with wide ribbons of a darker hue. The skirt, with only one flounce, was decorated with bows of the same wider ribbon and another of the bows was fastened in my hair, just behind my left ear. Altogether, I folt that I was complete to a shade and delighted in the occasion to practice my small talk without the possibility of being overset.

I overheard several of the older members of the party compliment Nick and Joan on having such a well-mannered sister to be presented to society and floated up the stairs to assemble myself for the trip back to Aunt Hattie's. It seemed as though I might take after all.

And then came Lady Melcourt's garden party. The aunts were determined that I should wear my hair up for a change and so my head was soaked in sugar water for the occasion. Aunt Kate's Jane had dredged up a memory from some far distant past and developed what at first trial appeared to be a workable idea. After using enough pins for several heads of hair, she then simply laid me back over a footstool and immersed the hair covered portion of my head in a strong solution of flower-scented sugar water. When it dried, it was so stiff, I declare that I could have gone into battle without a helmet.

We had tried this method only once, in the privacy of our home and it had worked wonderfully if you only consider that it did keep my hair where they wanted it. It also made my head itch most furiously and there was no way to scratch it. When I complained, I was told that certainly I could endure it for only one day and I promised to try. Of course, the garden party proved to be rather an unwise choice on our part, as so many birds and bees and other winged objects flocked to my head that we quite disrupted the party.

To complement my peach-colored silk gown, Jane had gathered some flowers from the garden in nearly the same shade and these she laboriously wove in and around various strands of my hair. When she had finished with them, she stood back and admired her handiwork. "You'll do," she said, a touch of pride in her voice. The aunts agreed and indeed, I was pleased as well. I'd never seen anything quite like this effect and thought the unusual touch very elegant indeed.

It was the end of May and lovely weather. The trees were almost in full leaf and the scent of spring flowers was everywhere in Lady Melcourt's substantial garden. One end of it was given to a large canopy, under which were chairs and little tables. Chairs had been placed here and there, adding up to a truly lovely sight. Waiters were busily bringing plates of sandwiches and cakes to accompany the iced lemonade and punch. There was a small orchestra in one corner under its own little canopy. I was entranced by the entire effect. Except for the trees and flowers everything was manmade but it had all been contrived with the utmost effort into a natural-appearing bower.

Tyler was there with Simon, Harry and Gareth. Past differences had all now been forgotten. Although I was now secure enough to be able to stand up and talk to those gentlemen, I did occasionally forget myself when presented to a newcomer. This one was named Jeremy. No sooner had Tyler made the introduction than, being somewhat taken aback, he took a step backward—into a footman, who unfortunately dropped his pitcher all over the boots of the other men. I reached to pick up the pitcher and bumped into Harry's thigh. My hair cracked. It still felt solid, though, so I didn't give it much thought right then. Eventually, with the help of Lord Melcourt's valet, the lemonade was removed from the boots, the footman admonished and sent back into the fray and we all rejoined the party. All except Jeremy, that is. He disappeared and I never saw him again.

Simon suggested a tour of the flowers and held out his arm to me. I felt very much the young lady of fashion with my hair in such a fashionable arrangement and silently, I blessed the aunts for their persistence. Tyler was there with Gareth and Harry so off we went. Even though I had lived in the country all my life and Hadleighwoode had lovely grounds, I had never seen such a variety of flowers. The roses alone were impressive but these were intermixed with peonies, poppies, lilies, iris and other fulsome blossoms I did not recognize. As I stopped to smell one particularly lovely rose, Simon said, "Don't move your head, Lady Bertie, there is a bee. Let me just get him out of your way."

I turned to thank him and Harry said, "There's another one. Lady Bertie, I think we should move to another area. The roses are evidently too much for the bees, today."

We all moved to another area of the garden enjoying the fresh warm air and the music. The aunts watched my progress, wearing smiles. We talked to several people that we had met on other occasions and Tyler introduced me to others. Occasionally we would stop for a glass of lemonade, not without reminiscent chuckles among us and we sampled the sandwiches and cakes. I was really having a wonderful time. We approached a small gathering which included Lady Colney. I decided to tell her, once again, how much I had enjoyed her musicale but as I came near enough to speak, she looked up at my head and screeched. Her mouth opened and closed like a fish but no words came out.

Tyler suddenly grabbed me and pulled me away. Indignantly I asked, "Just what do you think you are doing?" as he waved his arms around my head. Suddenly, my dearly loved brother attacked me! He began pulling the flowers out of my hair and throwing them on the ground around us. "Tyler!" I cried. "What are you doing? My hair will fall down if you are not careful. Please do not make me disgrace myself again, Tyler—"

"What do you have on your hair, Bertie?" he asked, as his arms still waved. His face was becoming red with his efforts. Dimly I realized that there were more birds chirping than I had noticed before. I looked up and nearly swooned. There was a veritable hive of bees as well as other flying creatures buzzing angrily around my head. These, in turn, were being challenged by the birds. It did not seem that the creatures were interested in each other, they were interested only in my head! I looked around at the rest of the party, who were all looking at me! *Not again*, I thought. Tyler jerked my arm and said, "Come along,

Bertie. We can't stand out here, we must get you indoors. Simon, give me your coat."

We rushed toward the house and suddenly I could see nothing. Tyler had thrown Simon's coat over my head to keep the birds and bees away from it. We went through the Melcourts' house and out the front door. "Gareth, go find the carriage. We'll take Bertie home and wash her hair. Whatever it is that is causing this little difficulty will certainly disappear with a little soap and water."

I said, "It's sugar water." Unfortunately because of the coat, Tyler couldn't hear me. He kept his arm around my shoulders as much to comfort me as to keep the coat in place. When I came to think on it later, he was very brave to take on all those birds and bees. He might have been injured. Bee stings are no fun as I know, having myself been stung at Hadleighwoode.

He patted my shoulder and made comforting noises. "We'll have you fixed up soon, brat." I could hear mumbling from the others but could not distinguish words. "Come Bertie, here is the carriage. Can you see the step? Ah good girl, in you go." He assisted me up into the carriage, in a not very gentlemanly fashion, I thought.

The five of us squeezed into the carriage, no easy trick I might say all of us being so large, but fortunately it was a short trip. When the carriage stopped Tyler said, "Simon, no Gareth you've still got your coat on, go and make sure the door is open so we can take Bertie straight inside and find the maid. We'll need her help."

In a moment Tyler said, "Bertie here we go. Keep Simon's coat over your head until we are through the doors, just in case. Once we are safely in the house we can remove it. We don't want to take any bees in with us. Harry, you keep a lookout for the little devils. Ready, then?" And I was half hustled, half carried into the house.

Once inside, Tyler removed the coat from my head. I looked around, semi-dazed. The four of them were standing around me with inquisitive looks on their faces. "I'm sorry Tyler. What in the world happened anyway?" I asked. I smiled at Simon. "Thank you for the loan of your coat Simon." His face turned red as he was trying to put his coat back on. "Tyler?"

"I don't know exactly, brat. All I can think of is that whatever perfume you had on your hair was just too much of an attraction for the bees who were too much of an attraction for the birds. I don't know."

"But there is no perfume on my hair. Or in it. Just flower-scented sugar water—"

"Sugar water?" asked Gareth.

"Sugar water on your hair?" gasped Tyler. "Flower-scented sugar water?"

"Oh my," said Harry.

Simon said nothing as he was still struggling with his coat.

"Sugar water," said I.

"What on earth possessed you to put sugar water on your hair?" I could sense the laughter starting to bubble up in Tyler as he asked the question.

"Well I didn't do it. You know that my hair will not hold a curl. Pins just fall out of it nearly as fast as you put them in. So Aunt Kate's maid Jane, remembered that several years ago when she encountered the same problem while in service elsewhere, she solved the problem with sugar water."

Tyler reached over to touch my hair. Disbelief was all over his face, temporarily replacing the laughter. "But this is marvelous!" He hit my hair. It crackled again. "I don't believe this," he hooted. "This is as good as armor any day!" He hit it again. "I say fellows, you have to try this. It's beyond anything!"

And so I stood there, patiently waiting for their high spirits to subside. It didn't hurt although it made a lot of noise. I was so grateful for the rescue I was willing to let them indulge in hitting my hair if they wished.

Their laughter soon brought Simpson and Jane to see what was happening. The looks on their faces soon had me laughing along with the younglings. I suppose it must have looked exceeding strange to see four brawny young men hitting the piled up hair of a young lady. Tyler spotted Jane and said, "Come, tell me how you do this."

Jane, with all the dignity only a superior servant can convey, said stiffly, "I'm sure I don't know what you mean, sir."

"I mean, how do you put sugar water on Bertie's hair and make it stay so," he explained. "And more important, how do you get it out? That's the most urgent question."

"You just wash it out sir, with soap and water. Come milady," she said to me, "I'll wash your hair for you right now. You could never be seen with it as it is." And she took me by the hand and started upstairs.

I turned around and said to Tyler, "Please wait for me, I won't be long. Please Tyler?"

"Go on brat, we'll wait, I promise. This is a story we have to hear and I think we're entitled to it all." He looked at Simpson. "Do the aunts have any whisky on the premises, Simpson? I think we'd all like a drink while we're waiting for m'sister."

Simpson, not as starchy as Bunford, grinned and said, "I think there is some kept for medicinal purposes, sir. If you'll please to come this way." He led them all away. Jane led me on upstairs, mumbling under her breath. I heard only, "I never—"

Once in my room, Jane set about getting everything she would need to dismantle my hair. I took off my pretty gown and covered myself with an old robe. I knew I should be fairly well drenched by the time she had finished her ministrations.

While she went down for the hot water, I removed as many pins as I could find. My hair never moved. I hit it with my fist and the noise it made reminded me of the younglings doing the same thing. In spite of my dismay at yet another social fiasco, I couldn't help but laugh.

As Jane came in with the hot water, I was standing in the middle of the room, hitting my hair and laughing. No wonder she looked at me so strangely! I didn't care. She soaked my head, then rinsed it. The cloying odor of sugar rose from the water. Another rinse, then the sweet smell of whatever soap she was using. Then another rinse. I was becoming waterlogged. Another soaping and yet another rinse and she pronounced me as ready to have my hair dried.

"There is no time!" I assured her. "I'll just put on a gown and go down as I am."

"You will not, miss!" she stated, as she grabbed a large towel and attacked my head. When she stopped to catch her breath, I threw the towel at her and ran to grab my gown.

"Jane, I simply must go down there. They might leave. I've just spent my last half hour in their company with a coat over my head. Surely, just being wet can not be as bad?"

Not waiting for her answer, I threw on a round gown and ran out the door and down the carpeted stairs. As I approached the drawing room, the door was ajar and I could hear their raucous laughter.

A voice I could not distinguish said, "I say, Tyler, that's famous!"

Another voice said, "He would be perfect for her. Most decidedly!"

Tyler's familiar voice said, "Then you'll all come? He'll meet us there."

The first voice said, "I had thought he was to meet us today?"

As I have previously stated, I know I should not be listening outside doors but this one was open, at least a little and sometimes one does hear the most interesting things. I stood there, not making any noise at all. I was hardly breathing.

"I think we all left too early," said the first voice.

There was laughter and then, "Can't you just see it?" I thought that was Simon, or maybe Gareth.

"I don't know why I never thought of it before," Tyler was laughing so hard he could barely talk.

I must have made a noise, because they suddenly all became quiet. Putting a smile on my face to replace the confusion, I entered the room. They had all removed their jackets and were relaxed and happy.

"Back so soon, brat?" Tyler asked. He patted the sofa beside him. "Come sit here and tell us about the sugar water."

They made a wonderful audience, listening and laughing. I had not felt so comfortable in such a long time that I quite forgot myself and after the final chuckles had died away I asked, "Tyler, who's coming to Hadleighwoode? In addition to all of you, that is?" I looked around the room, including all of them in my question, though I spoke primarily to Tyler.

There was immediate silence in the room and I mentally cursed myself and my busy mouth. To cover my mistake, I said brightly, "I had heard Nick mention that someone might visit, I think. Is your 'he' and Nick's the same, do you suppose?"

A strangled sound came from Harry. I looked at him and caught the most bewildered expression on his face. When I looked back at Tyler, his face also had an impenetrable look. Tyler seemed to accept my explanation as he answered, "I can't say that for sure. We were just talking about another one of our usual rackety set. I don't think you've been in the way of meeting him yet — or at least not lately."

Simon cleared his throat and in an obvious attempt to change the subject, asked, "Have you been to Vauxhall yet, Lady Bertie?"

Gareth, ever helpful, followed with, "And how about the Tower or the Royal Academy, or —?"

Harry was not to be left out. "Do you expect to go to Almack's? You must save me a dance, when you do go."

I may not be a bluestocking but even I could tell that no further information about this mysterious "he" would be forthcoming.

Tyler rose to his feet. "Oh tell me you're not leaving?" I pleaded. "I haven't enjoyed myself so much for ages. And I wanted to ask you —"

"All good things must come to an end, puss, and we must be elsewhere. Aunt Kate and Aunt Hattie will no doubt be home, soon. You won't be alone for long."

The other three stood up and they took turns helping each other into their tightly fitting jackets. It was fascinating to watch. I suppose that according to society I should not have been watching, as it was considered not the done thing for a young lady to even see a gentleman without his jacket but I no longer cared much for society, as it was obvious society had not cared overmuch for me, either.

They all smiled at me but I surprised them by saying, "I think that when next we meet, it must be at Hadleighwoode. After this afternoon, I cannot imagine that I will be very welcome anywhere."

Tyler came and put his arms around me. "Don't fret so, puss. The season will soon be over and by next autumn, no one will remember. You can begin again."

We all trooped out into the hall where we were met by Simpson. "Do you wish me to find you a hackney coach, sir?" he asked Tyler.

"No, I think we'll walk. It's such a fine evening and we've not far to go" He kissed my cheek. The others, in turn, solemnly took my hand and kissed it and then they were gone. The tears started down my cheek.

"There, miss. I'll bring you a nice cup of tea," said Simpson.

I shocked that gentleman by saying, "I think I'd rather have a whisky, Simpson. I'm going to need it when the aunts arrive." But I didn't have the whisky or the tea, either. I trudged up the stairs and into my room where I flung myself on the bed and proceeded to have a lovely long cry, followed by an unplanned nap.

Chapter Six

ॐ

The boat was rocking violently and I was certain we should all be tipped into the sea. "It was not my fault," I shouted. Someone was shaking my shoulder. Were they purposely trying to tip me overboard? I flung out my arm and heard a startled "Umphh!"

"My lady please wake up." Jane was shaking me more gently now.

I opened my eyes and discovered that I was on my bed, not in a boat after all. I peered up at Jane through my sleepy fog. "What? Jane, why are you—?"

"My lady, your brother and the countess are downstairs with Miss Kate and Miss Hattie." Jane's voice dropped to a hoarse whisper as she said those two portentous words, "the countess". I shuddered. "They wish you to join them. Come now and rinse your face and put on a fresh gown. That one you're wearing is a fright!" She went over to the wardrobe and began to rummage around in it.

"Could you please say that I am too ill to come down?" I pleaded but with not much hope.

"No, miss. I was told that you must appear and so you shall," she answered briskly. Jane set about making me presentable, at least on the outside. I was not looking forward to this occasion and made up my mind that no matter what anyone said, I should return to Hadleighwoode as soon as humanly possible. If Nick would not let me use one of his carriages then I would rent one. I would use some of the guineas given to me as extra pin money by Aunt Cassie before I left for London. This thought cheered me a bit.

I expected Joan to be in fine fettle. She didn't disappoint me.

I had barely entered the room when she turned on me. Without even a hello, she went right to the heart of the matter. "Whatever can have possessed you to behave in such a disgraceful fashion yet again?" she all but screeched at me.

"I—" I was interrupted.

"Come over here and sit. I cannot always be looking up at you. Sit there!" She pointed to the most uncomfortable and smallest chair in the room. Sitting in that chair had resulted in my knees coming entirely too close to my chin for comfort as well as breathing, so I had avoided that chair ever since and started to do so again. She grabbed my arm and headed me in the direction of the detested thing.

"Sit!" she commanded and pushed me down into it.

She was truly magnificent, nearly breathing fire. I was sure I could smell the brimstone. "How can you continually do such stupid things? If you had set out to discommode me, you could not have done better." She stalked about the room.

"But Joan," Aunt Kate was trying to defend me, I hoped.

"I didn't ask you, I asked Zenobia." Joan looked at me. I would like to know how she manages to speak so clearly when her jaw is so tightly clenched. It would seem to be painful but it didn't seem to bother her very much. Or slow her down, either. "Well, miss? I am waiting for your explanation." Her small foot tapped the floor with impatience.

"I think it was the sugar water," I began hesitantly.

"What has sugar water to do with anything?" she interrupted.

"Aunt Joan, I am—"

"Don't call me aunt. I am not your aunt!"

I was startled into submission as I looked up at her. It was entirely true. Joan was not my aunt. I was so used to being surrounded by aunts that I had fallen into the habit of calling her such. I took a deep breath and began again.

"My hair just will not—"

"I care nothing for your hair." She snapped her finger as she sneered the words at me. "What did you do to Lady Colney? That is what I want to know. She was in such a state she could only mutter something about 'birds and bees'. What did you say to her to give her such fits?" Joan was still pacing the floor and she really did resemble nothing so much as a ferocious animal.

"I have been trying to tell you, A—Joan. It was my hair. But the incident itself was not my fault. Well I suppose it was my fault, as was my hair. But how were we to know that the bees would be attracted by the flowers, or the sugar water and congregate so about my head? And then the birds—"

The strangest noise was coming from Nick. I stopped my narrative and looked over at him. His face was so red I feared he was having an apoplexy. He rose from his chair and went to the nearest window and began to open it. He stopped and looked over at me. "I trust that the sugar water is now dispensed with and I may safely open the window without fear of further attack?" He raised the window and gulped in great breaths of the fresh evening air. It seemed a wonderful idea to me and I tried to get out of my chair to go and join him.

Joan pushed me back again. For a small woman she had an amazing amount of strength and as the chair tipped backward, I feared for a moment that we might go over completely. Just what I needed.

"It was only an attempt to make my hair into a fashionable look, Joan. Until I stopped to smell that rose everything was as it should be. Perhaps I disturbed a hive, or maybe it was Simon and Harry waving the bees away that brought more of them to the rescue of their friends. I do not know. The only thing I do know is that I have never been so miserable in my life. I only wish to go home to

Hadleighwoode. If this is the way that other young ladies find husbands then I shall remain unwed!" Tears that had remained in my eyes during that speech, a rather long one for me, at least when in Joan's presence, now began their trek down my cheeks. "Please, Nick," I appealed to him, "let me go back home."

Nick looked at Joan. The silence in the room became oppressive. I struggled to get out of the infernal chair. Finally I stood upright and walked toward the door. "I shall go you know, whatever you say. I still have enough guineas from Aunt Cassie to hire a coach. I will not stay in this miserable place one more day." My voice was beginning to be very unstable. "I have no wish to be a lady. I just want to be me."

Holding my head high I ran out of the room and up the stairs again. Once in my room, I began to pull my clothes out of the wardrobe and fling them on the bed. Somewhere in here must be my carpetbag. I would take only what I could carry. Aunt Hattie could send the rest of my things later in my trunk. My eyes were still blurred with tears and occasionally I sobbed aloud. There was a gentle tap on my door.

"Go away. You will not change my mind. I will go home, I will."

"Bertie, please open the door to me." It was Nick. "Let me come in and talk to you for just a minute. Please Bertie?" His comforting voice barely came through the door.

"Is Joan with you?" I called.

"No. No one is with me. Please let me in."

I went and opened the door and as Nick came into the room he held out his arms to me. I threw myself into them and began to sob once more.

"Here now. I never knew you to be such a watering pot," he said, as he gently blotted my face with his handkerchief. "Bertie, I promise you I had no intention of ever hurting you. You were the one who wanted to come up to London and I

103

only wanted to give you whatever I could that might make you happy. Come, sit down and let's discuss this a little."

My sobs receded slightly and I looked at him. My wonderful big brother-father combination, steady as the Rock of Gibraltar which he so greatly resembled. "Hush, now dear one, don't cry anymore. You do not need to stay here if you truly do not wish to do so. I will send my carriage for you in the morning and you can go back to Hadleighwoode. No more tears?" He offered me the handkerchief to finish my mopping up. "Perhaps you might wish to come back in the fall—?"

"No, Nick. I do not wish to ever see London again. Do I really have to get married? Is it so awful for me to just stay at Hadleighwoode? Oh please Nick, say I may just stay there. Please!"

"Hush dear. For now, just let us send you back to Hadleighwoode on a repairing lease shall we say? And we simply won't worry about the future right now. How is that? We won't even think about society, I promise you."

Dear Nick, he was the most comforting person in my life. "Just think," he said, "in two days you shall be with Bessie, again."

Bessie! In all my trials I had nearly forgotten her. How could I have done such a thing? What had she been doing while I was gone? The next days would not pass quickly enough to suit me. I threw my arms around Nick's neck and kissed him solidly on his cheek.

* * * * *

Whether it was the wonderful comfort of Nick's carriage, or simply a release of the tension that had surrounded me in London, or a combination of the two, I slept nearly all the way home to Hadleighwoode. The homing instinct in me must be strong because I awakened refreshed less than a mile from the gates. I looked out the windows, first one side then the other, drinking in the familiar surroundings. The soft Kent countryside never looks lovelier than in the period of dusk. The rosy glow of the sun lends a dreamlike quality that, when coupled with the green and gold of the rolling hills, tugs at my head and my heart as no other place that I have ever seen.

If I had anything to say about my future—and I did know that it was by no means certain that I would have—I should never leave Hadleighwoode again. Well perhaps for a day or so now and then but no longer. I intended to plant my substantial feet and grow roots. I was so anxious that I was out of the carriage and nearly at the front door before Millett, our butler, had opened it.

The poor man! He had been with our family since before I was born but I am sure that he had never been so shocked as he was then, to find himself on the receiving end of my exuberant hug and the firm buss on his cheek. "Millett! Oh it is so good to be back home. I shall never leave again!" I disentangled us and danced across the hall.

"Where is everyone? Is Bessie in the stables? My aunts?" I was too excited to proceed.

"Er, ah, welcome home, Lady Bertie, I'm sure." Good old Millett had never been near the starch bucket in his life. A huge grin appeared on his face and he clasped my hand in his, as I danced back over to him. "We're that pleased to have you home again, miss. Your aunts are in the parlor, I believe and Lady Bessie—"

"Never mind, Millett, I'll find them all myself." I threw my bonnet up in the air and exclaimed, "Oh it is so good to be back home!" I ran down the hall past the drawing room, noticed that the door was open and caught just a brief, fleeting glimpse of a very petite and attractive young woman in a glorious pink confection of a gown. I didn't immediately recognize her, but I was too anxious to find Bessie and the aunts to go back for a better look.

I burst into the parlor and there indeed were the aunts. Dear Aunt Cassie and Aunt Penny, looking more like the twins that one would imagine when hearing the word, came to greet me.

"Bertie, my dear—"

"Oh my love—"

"It is so wonderful—" We were all speaking at one time and tangling arms together in our attempts at hugs. Finally, we compromised on a three-way hug and just stood there. I finally stepped out of their embraces and said, "Oh why can I never find my handkerchief when I need it?" Tears, this time of joy, were once again streaming down my face but this time it was such a relief to not have to care about my looks.

Aunt Penny gave me her minute, lace-trimmed excuse for a handkerchief and patted my other hand. Aunt Cassie went looking for her vinaigrette. I sat down and heaved what must have been the largest sigh of my existence to date. I smiled at both aunts and proclaimed, "I will never leave Hadleighwoode again. Never."

"Was it so horrid, then?" Aunt Cassie asked.

"You must tell us all about it," was Aunt Penny's comment. Looks of perplexity and confusion crossed their lovely vague faces.

"I will. Never fear, you shall both hear all about it. But first I must find Bessie." I started toward the door leading out to the terrace and from where I could easily walk to the stable. "She promised to write to me but I should have realized she would not."

"But Bertie—" Aunt Penny began.

"I promise you I will tell you everything but I have to find Bessie. I won't be long, I assure you." And I continued toward the door.

To my immense surprise, Aunt Cassie ran across the room and grabbed my arm. "But that's what we've been trying to tell you love. She isn't in the stable."

"What, Bessie not in the stable? Has she gone somewhere, then? Oh I suppose that there is a sick animal somewhere that she has gone to tend?" I replied, saddened by the thought that my reunion with Bessie would be further delayed.

"No dear, she is in the parlor."

Bessie in the parlor? Bessie? This was hard to believe. "But when I passed the door, I saw only a young lady in a pink gown." I stopped in confusion. "Never say that was Bessie?" I ran out of the room and back to the parlor. The young lady was standing in silhouette in front of one of the windows. She appeared to be what Tyler would surely have called "a diamond of the first water". "Oh I beg your pardon, miss. I was looking for my sister—" My jaw dropped, prohibiting further words, as the young lady turned into the light and crossed over to me.

"You goose, Bertie. You have found your sister." My knees became so weak that I fell into a nearby chair. The vision in pink came over and with one delicate and very clean finger slowly raised my lower jaw back up into its proper position.

"Bessie," I breathed. "Is it really you?" I had never in my life been so astonished.

"Of course it's me," she chortled. "Do you not like my gown?" And she whirled around for my inspection, accompanied by her giggles.

"Aunt Cassie," I whispered.

"Is that all you have to say?" Bessie asked.

"Her vinaigrette. I finally have need of it. Or burning feathers. Or something. Bessie what in the world has happened to you? I would have never known you. Never!"

"I'm in love, Bertie and it is the most wonderful thing! Just wait until it happens to you and you will know what I mean. It makes you do the strangest things!"

I could well believe that statement just by looking at her. Her mop of curls was held back from her face by a pink ribbon which exactly matched the ones on her gown. And that gown! Bessie had the kind of figure for which that style had been created. She would have set London on its collective ear without a moment's doubt, to my mind at least.

Joan would have been ecstatic over Bessie in this gown. She was perfect. I was still too stunned to speak. My world had turned upside down. I knew in that moment that my comfortable safe haven at Hadleighwoode would never again be the same but the feeling of sadness at that thought was mingled with my happiness for Bessie.

"No wonder you didn't write to me. Who is he? Do you plan to marry? How did you meet him?" I had suddenly found my voice.

Bessie sat on the arm of the chair and grinned at me. "His name is Malcolm Ferguson and he is the Baron Silverton. Yes we plan to marry, in the autumn and we met…" She giggled again and was once more the hoydenish Bessie I remembered. "I was in the stable in my usual garb, tending Blanket." Blanket was our first grown-up horse. Well past her prime, we refused to relinquish her for fear of her ending up at someplace too horrible even to contemplate. Bessie regularly tended Blanket, making sure she got the tender food she needed now that the mare's poor old worn teeth could not cope with her regular food. "I thought that Robin was in the stable. I heard someone yell but I paid no attention when suddenly I was swatted on my, er, behind. I turned around to see who would do such a thing and there he was. My hat had fallen off and I had removed my jacket. Up so close he could easily see that I wasn't a boy and he was so embarrassed."

She giggled again, remembering. "I don't know which of us was more startled. There was this dandy, or so I thought, dressed in the height of fashion and here was I dressed like a stable boy but obviously not one. His face went all red and he stammered, 'I do beg your pardon, miss. I thought you were the stable hand.' I rubbed my, er, behind and his face got even more red. Actually, it almost matched his hair. His hair flames it is so red. And his eyes are the most glorious blue, just like the morning-glories by the side of the stable." A dreamy look passed over her face, accompanied by a singularly sweet smile.

"It seems he really did want me, after all. But at that time, he was just looking for a stable hand to take his mount." She paused for a moment. "You see, he has a small stable and has entered his best goer in a race. The poor horse had come up lame during a practice and he was directed to me for an herbal poultice. Dear Mal, he never expected to find me out there." Bessie came to a halt, lost in her memories.

"And then what happened?" I prompted.

"It was like being struck by lightning, Bertie. For both of us at the same time. He rides over here nearly every day."

"And do you wear such a gown every day?"

"Oh no, you goose. We are going to a party at Hamden. I was just waiting for him to come and collect me." She looked at me with an expression on her face that I could not like. "Bertie, this is famous! If you would make yourself presentable you could come with us. I am sure that Mal would not mind in the least."

This was entirely too much for me to take in. Here was I, in an exceedingly fashionable day dress of the utmost style, at least by London standards, being told by my sister, who was usually to be found in breeches, to go and make myself presentable. No wonder I was all about in my head. It was spinning entirely too much for coherent thought.

"No, my love, I think not. I would much prefer to stay at home this evening and adjust to being home again, if such a thing is possible." I shook my head in wonder. "I think I shall need several days to sort this out. You go as planned and have a wonderful time." I paused as a vagrant thought stopped in my head for a moment. "Do you dance, Bessie?" I asked.

"Well of course. Why should you ask such a silly question? It is the most fun!" As if to demonstrate, she stood up and began to dance with an imaginary partner, swooping and whirling around the room. Holding my head, I groaned. Immediately Bessie was back at my side.

"Bertie, are you all right?" she asked, her face full of concern for me.

"Yes, I think I am." I smiled up at her. "Actually everything has been happening so quickly that I am not truly sure, but yes, I think so."

"Mal should be here soon but until then, you must tell me about all the exciting things you saw and did in London," Bessie said. "Did you go to many balls and parties? Were you to Almack's? Is it as wonderful and exciting as they say it is?"

I groaned again. "Bessie, London was awful beyond anything I ever dreamed. I could do nothing right. Joan has washed her hands of me. It seemed as though every time I went anywhere I caused a riot. I never wish to go to London again, ever. I shall just simply stay here at Hadleighwoode." I looked at her and grinned. "And anyway, look at you. You stayed and found a husband right here. Who says husbands may be found only in London?"

Bessie grinned back at me and I knew that nothing could ever part us, not husbands or miles. It was so good to be home again. I pulled her down onto my lap and we hugged as we were used to do. She endured the hug for only a moment before jumping up and saying with a mischievous look, "Could we continue that tomorrow? It did feel good but I don't want to crease my gown."

"Bessie!" I exclaimed. "That is the outside of enough. I never, ever thought I should live so long as to hear those words from you. Crease your gown, indeed." Before I could say more, Millett came into the room.

"Baron Silverton is here, miss," he said.

Bessie clapped her hands together in glee. "Show him in, Millett." She suddenly became a stylish young lady right before my eyes. I started to rise out of the chair. "Oh no, Bertie, please remain seated."

Malcolm Ferguson, the Baron Silverton, came into the room and I knew why Bessie told me to remain in my chair. The baron was a perfect miniature of a Greek God. From the indeed flaming red hair down to his gleaming black Hessians, he was proportioned to Bessie as no one I had ever seen. She rushed to him and I noticed that he topped her five feet by not more than two or three inches. Love was all over his face and I could well believe Bessie's claim of lightning having struck. I might have been invisible for all the notice they took of me.

Holding hands, he kissed her gently on the cheek and they murmured sweet nothings to each other. After several minutes of this, Bessie remembered me. "Mal my dear, I should like to present to you my twin, my dearly loved sister Bertie. Don't mind if she doesn't get up. She is exhausted from her trip home from London. She has not been here above an hour." Bessie may have been small in inches but she was large in love. It was almost of a touchable quality as it surrounded all of us.

Malcolm came over and took the hand I held up to him. "It is most wonderful to meet you, Lady Bertie, as I have heard so much of you from Bessie and the aunts," he said. "I am pleased to have you for a sister, as I have none of my own."

"Do you have brothers, then, Baron Silverton?" I asked. I was totally charmed by him. He was quite the most adorable little thing I had ever seen, next to Bessie, of course. I could have picked him up and carried him around as one does a pet, with his broad shoulders, trim waist and muscular thighs but yet all so marvelously proportioned to his small frame!

"I wish you would call me Malcolm, or Mal as your sweet sister does." He smiled at Bessie. Oh to have someone smile at me in that way. "But to answer your question, yes, I have three older brothers, great huge fellows they are too. I am by way of being the runt of the litter, so to speak. They are all older than me by some years. Actually they are half brothers, as my father married again after their mother, who was his first wife, died. I am the only child of that second marriage." He was absolutely at his ease, standing there calmly discussing his lineage.

"You are probably wondering how I, as the youngest son, am called the Baron Silverton."

"Bertie, it is the most wonderful story," Bessie interrupted him. He only patted her hand.

"My mother had one brother who had no heir but his lands were not entailed. When Mama died I was still quite young and so I went to live with Uncle Jonas. He became determined that I should inherit and instructed me in the management of his estates. For many years I was certain that he was my real father. Certainly no one could have been more like one. He even thought at one time of adopting me but my real father balked. Since the title would come to me anyway, through Mama, it proved to be unnecessary. My ancestral seat is in Scotland but Mama was English. Except for my name and my hair, there is very little in me that is not English. I was pleased to have a home of my own here in England. Silverton is less than half an hour's ride from here. You must ride over with Bessie one day. When you are rested from your trip, of course," he added politely.

"Isn't it amazing, Bertie, how similar our backgrounds are, with only older brothers and everyone else in the family so lar—" She stopped talking, confusion on her face. It became obvious to me that she had not told him all that much about me. "Mal, dear, perhaps we should be leaving, so dear Bertie can get her rest."

Malcolm smiled at her and then at me. As I held up my hand to him, I asked, "Have you met any of our brothers, yet?"

"Oh Bertie, I forgot to tell you that. He bought a horse from Jon and Mary Anne and that's why he came here for the poultice. Isn't that wonderful?"

She tucked her arm in his and gently led him to the door. "Bertie, you must rest after your trip. We will not be late home, though." She detached herself from him and ran back to kiss me goodbye.

"Have a marvelous time, you two!" I called to them as they went, laughing, out of the door. My head was spinning with all this new information to digest. I had never thought I'd see Bessie as a young lady in love. However, it was a delightful sight and I was truly happy for her.

* * * * *

Bessie was more correct than she knew. I was suddenly so tired I could hardly hold my head upright. My lower limbs seemed to be made of water and when I tried to rise from the chair I could not. A sudden noise startled me and I was surprised to see the aunts hovering over me.

"We couldn't find you, Bertie," Aunt Cassie said.

"Were you having a little nap?" this from Aunt Penny.

"I suddenly found myself so tired I could not get out of this chair. I think I must get to my bed or I will find myself right here in the morning," I replied.

"Country air, when you are not used to it, does make one extremely sleepy. I have observed that myself. Haven't you, Penny?" Aunt Cassie held out a hand to me. "Come, dear, Penny and I will help you to your room. A good night's sleep will set things right for you, you'll see." Each of them took one of my hands, tugged gently to get me on my feet and we made our slow progress up the stairs. I had not anticipated being so touched at the sight of my room but all my childhood memories came flooding back, producing tears once again.

"Oh," I exclaimed. "I am turning into a first-class watering pot. But it is so good to be back home. I swear I shall never leave again." The aunts just looked at each other and smiled. Aunt Cassie bustled around, turning back the covers on my huge bed and closing the curtains at the windows, while Aunt Penny pushed my fumbling fingers aside and undid the buttons on my dress. "Would you like a cup of tea or chocolate, or a glass of milk, my dear? It may help you to sleep," she said.

"No thank you, I don't think I could stay awake long enough to drink it." My eyelids were closing even as I stood there. With their help I climbed into my bed and drew up the covers. I did not even hear them leave the room.

Sunlight on my face woke me. I sat up, startled. Only late morning sun ever came into my room. What on earth had happened to me? I had never slept so long at one time before in my entire life. I rang for Mary and promptly fell asleep again. The rattle of a tea tray finally penetrated my unconscious state. I pushed myself up on my pillows. "Welcome home, my lady. Here is your tea." Mary set the tray down on the table beside my bed and went to open the drapes. Aunt Cassie had left one window partly open and I could feel the warmth of the sun that was streaming in. As Mary opened each drapery the room became lighter. I poured myself a cup of tea and looked around at the familiar and much-loved room. "Would you like a bath, my lady? We have water heating for you and it's no trouble to bring it up."

"Yes, Mary, I think I should. I had no time last evening." I remembered then about Bessie and her Malcolm. "Where is Bessie?" I asked.

"Out in the stables, as usual, miss," Mary answered.

"In the stables?"

"Yes, miss. She is still there nearly all the time, just like she always was." Mary was standing at the doorway. "Let me bring your bath water. Would you like me to send for Lady Bessie?"

"No, leave her. I'll find her once I have bathed and dressed." I was now awake and wondering what else was happening in my beloved little world of Hadleighwoode. The bath was refreshing and I hurriedly dressed and went downstairs. The familiar faces of the servants expressed their pleasure at my return. I greeted each of them, accepting their love. Oh it was good to be back!

I set off on a tour of the house. An inner compulsion drove me to inspect each room to assure myself that nothing had changed. The gardens drew me outdoors and I breathed deeply of the perfumed air. If nothing else had been accomplished by my futile trip to London at least I should now be able to fully appreciate my home as I had never before been able to do. For me the greenest grass would always be that at Hadleighwoode. I looked over to the stables and there was Bessie, as I was used to seeing her, in breeches and shirt with a cap pulled down over her curls.

She was leading a large horse around the paddock. It seemed to be favoring its left forefoot. After a few steps, she would stop and give the horse a pat on the face and a small treat that was daintily nuzzled from her open hand. I could not hear her but I could see her lips moving in gentle words of encouragement, which were answered by the horse nuzzling her hand and butting her in the chest with his head. She laughed in enjoyment. A small figure came around the far end of the stable and Bessie called to him. It was Malcolm!

I stood there, stunned by his presence, which didn't seem to bother Bessie at all. I decided to go over to them and see what they were doing. He could not remain in ignorance of my inches for much longer and now was as good a time as any for the disclosure.

They were engrossed in their discussion of the horse, taking turns at inspecting and rubbing its leg and talking to it, when I joined in.

"Good morning, or is it afternoon?" I said, brightly.

Bessie whirled around with a startled look on her face.

"I believe it is now afternoon, Lady Bertie-e-e," Malcolm's voice died away as his gaze rose from my chest to my face, paling as it went. He swallowed, flashed a look at Bessie and continued in somewhat of a croak, "Are you feeling more the thing today, then?"

"Yes, indeed I am," I responded in a determinedly cheerful manner. "I had not realized how truly worn out I was. Bessie was right as I was even compelled to have a short nap in my chair before I was able to travel up to my room." I looked around and added, "I knew it would not take long before Hadleighwoode worked its restoring miracle." Glancing at the horse which was still nuzzling Bessie, I asked, "Is this the one you brought to Bessie's care, Malcolm?"

Bessie found her voice. "Yes, isn't he beautiful? His name is Silverton's Pride and he is to run at the Derby next month if we get his leg to work properly."

He was indeed beautiful, a light gray all over, not dappled as grays usually are. Although not a heavy horse, he was tall and Bessie and Mal barely came to the top of his shoulder. Mal patted the horse on the neck.

"If he recovers enough to run and should win I plan to breed him to the mare I purchased from your brother Jon. I think their offspring—" He lowered his head and shuffled his feet. "I do beg your pardon, Lady Bertie, I forgot myself. I should not be discussing such topics in your presence." His face was losing its flush.

"But if you can discuss such topics with Bessie, sir, then surely you may include me?"

"I would not wish to offend you. I was told that your interests were more with matters inside the home rather than in the stable. Bessie, now—" He turned to look at her and grinned. "I am so used to her being underfoot out here that I do not watch what I say at all."

Bessie grinned back at him and said, "And you would not believe some of what I've heard either." She punched him in the shoulder as she said this.

He turned to look at her and she punched him again. She dropped the reins and took off in a run across the yard. Malcolm looked at me in consternation and with a shrug took off after her. Their yips and yells filled the air. Timidly, I reached out a hand and patted the neck of Silverton's Pride. He made a soft rumbling noise, almost like a cat's purring sound. I addressed him, "It's certainly easy to see how important we are, my fine fellow!" He thrust his head up and down several times as if to agree with my words.

Flushed and panting, Bessie and Malcolm, hand in hand, rejoined us. Bessie again took up the reins and Malcolm looked happily at her. "One of these days, miss, I shall catch you and throw you in the water trough!"

"Ah-hah!" said Bessie. "You'll have to catch me first!"

It was only too obvious that my presence was *de trop*, so with a smile I took my leave of them and returned to the house.

Chapter Seven

ဢ

In less than a week it was as though I had never been away. Oh there were some small differences—the daily presence of Malcolm and the absence of Nick and Joan's children, who were off to visit with their maternal grandparents. I fell back into the easy, comfortable routine of Hadleighwoode and luxuriated in it.

I had been responsible for much hearty laughter as I regaled the aunts and Bessie and Malcolm with the tales of my abbreviated visit to London. From the vantage point of time, I was able to see for myself the hilarity in some of these tales and my own laughter helped to cleanse the unpleasantness from my memories.

Bessie was most disappointed that I had not visited that "holy of holies", Almack's, and I wondered if she was now wishing she had gone with me. Considering Bessie's lack of polish, I felt that she might indeed do much better after marriage with Malcolm at her side.

There was only one small item to distress me. That is even too strong a word to explain the thoughts of the giant who occasionally wandered into my mind and, more occasionally, into my dreams. I tried to banish him but with not much success. Perhaps when Tyler and his friends came I should be able to find out who he was. His very size made him appealing and unappealing at the same time. My mind whirled with such mixtures of feelings that I became ever more determined to try to erase him from it.

In my short time in London, I had discovered that to most men, a woman was considered to be little more than an ornament and wives were chosen with this attribute as the most desired quality. The only exceptions were those where the dowry was uppermost. Nick would never countenance a marriage for me where my dowry was the prime consideration. I could not imagine myself as an ornament. Other than my brothers—and the giant—I had never seen any man whom I could serve in the position of an ornament, so with sadness I decided to learn to live with my renewed decision to remain unwed.

I should learn everything that I could from all of my aunts, the good and the bad and perfect for myself the art of being an aunt. It would be no hardship for me to remain at Hadleighwoode in that capacity and after a few days of such thoughts, I felt that I could successfully make such a life for myself. At least, I would try.

The more I saw of Malcolm the more I came to love him. It would have made no difference to Bessie, however, whatever my feelings should have been. She was so besotted with him she would not have cared if he suddenly sprouted wings or horns or a tail. He adjusted quickly to my size and within that week, became as dear to me as if he had always been part of our family. I could not think that Nick and Joan could find him unacceptable in any way. I wondered how he would feel surrounded by yet another family so much larger than he was.

Bessie had decided to be married from the little church in our village, rather than have a big London wedding and had already visited the local seamstress. A wonderfully frilly confection of white silk and lace was already being constructed, as well as all of the various items of clothing necessary to the social life of a baroness. Such a large order was not a commonplace occurrence to the seamstress and she treated Bessie with all the deference usually accorded to a duchess. For Bessie, it was like being exposed to an entirely new world and I was continually amazed at her enjoyment of it.

Her talk now consisted of such unfamiliar words as "flowers", "ribbons", "lace" and "flounces" or "ruffles", instead of the more common, for her, "fetlock", "withers", "spavined" and such. It was all wonderful fun. There were times, however, when it all became too much for her and she would dash out of the room. Shortly after, the old Bessie would reappear almost as if by magic, garbed in her old breeches and shirt along with her usual insouciance, as she ran out to the stables.

And then one day we heard the sounds of horses approaching and discovered Tyler and the younglings had come for their promised visit. Bessie was trying on one of her new gowns and the sight of her garbed thusly quite silenced Tyler. It was evident that if he had come upon her unawares, as I did, he would not have recognized her either. The other three were struck dumb at her appearance and stood, uncomfortable and uncertain. I nearly laughed out loud at the sight.

Tyler recovered his voice to croak at her, "Never say that this is Bessie? This vision of loveliness cannot be the grubby hoyden I remember?"

"Of course it is, you great looby!" she whispered demurely, looking up at him. A wicked grin flashed across her face and she suddenly threw herself up into his arms. Miraculously he caught her and whirled around the room with her in his embrace. Carefully he set her down, holding her hands in his as he backed up slightly for a better look.

The other three gentlemen, the aunts and I all stood there watching, trying to suppress laughter at their pleasure. A frown replaced the smile on Tyler's face as he turned to look at his friends. "It appears that I am a liar, my friends," he said, with a devil glinting in his blue eyes. "But this little minx is indeed my sister Bessie, although it is hard to tell without the usual dabs of grime on her face and without her breeches!" Bessie's face turned red as she pulled her hand from his. Words struggled to come but finally giving up the effort, she ran from the room.

"Tyler!" I admonished him, rather more sharply than I was used to doing. "That was not at all kind in you. Bessie is still unsure of herself in such garb and you have not endeared yourself to her with your remark." I turned to face the young men and softened my voice. "But I am as much at fault as you, having forgotten my manners and not acknowledged our guests, whom I remember with much fondness. Nor have we reintroduced them to our aunts!"

There was a deal of greetings and introductions back and forth, punctuated by the sound of a door slamming upstairs. I sighed, "There goes Bessie, out to her more silent and accepting friends." Tyler had the grace to look embarrassed as he said to me, "But why is Bessie so involved in gowns? How have you ever managed to—?"

"Not I, my dear, but Malcolm Ferguson, the Baron Silverton. Our little Bessie will become his baroness this fall," I explained, laughing at the expression on Tyler's face.

"Silverton?" asked Simon, with a thoughtful expression on his face. "I say, Tyler, you remember him? Has a stable of some of the finest bloods in these parts." He looked at me. "That is who you mean, isn't it, Lady Bertie?"

I nodded my assent. "He should be here soon. He visits us nearly every day and if he doesn't come here, then Bessie goes there." I could not resist adding, with an impish look at Tyler, "It seems a bolt of lightning, or some such—"

Gareth interrupted me with, "He's never been much in the petticoat line, as I remember. Raised by an uncle or some such, I seem to recall."

Harry mused, "Once lost a race to the little devil. He's a real neck or nothing rider but has a great advantage in his size."

Tyler clapped a hand to his forehead. "Pint-sized little squirt? With red hair? Once mistook him for a stableboy—"

My chortle of laughter interrupted him. "You'll never believe this but that is exactly how they met. He mistook Bessie for a stableboy and swatted her on the…well, in an improper place, because she didn't answer his calls!"

The five of us dissolved in laughter. I felt a tug at my sleeve and turned to see the anxious face of Aunt Cassie looking up at me. "My dears, you must not be unkind to Bessie and Malcolm just because they are not giants like the rest of you. They are perfectly suited to one another." Her serious words brought us back to ourselves.

Tyler took her hand and that of Aunt Penny. "Not to worry, my dears. I wouldn't tangle with that young worthy for anything. They may be small but I beg to inform you that even his muscles have muscles. I've seen him at Gentleman Jackson's in town. I would place my bet on Silverton, no matter who his opponent might be, I do assure you!"

Simon added, "Yes, that is a certainty. Never saw anyone who strips to advantage as well as Silverton. Rest on it, ma'am, he is highly regarded by the sporting set."

Harry was not to be left out of this discussion either. "Not just the sporting set, y'know. Everyone I know holds him in great affection. Good brainbox too. Graduated with honors from Oxford. Your Miss Bessie could not be in better hands."

Aunt Penny smiled at them well aware that Nicholas would not have approved the marriage if it was not a suitable one. "I'm glad to hear it from you, young sirs. Now, shall we have tea, or would you rather lemonade? I'm sure you must be parched after your ride."

We agreed on lemonade and Millett soon brought in the tray. After we had all been served, Tyler began to pace the room in a restless manner. "I think I must go and mend my fences with Bessie. Truly, I did not mean to hurt her. I was only so surprised." He replaced his glass on the tray and walked out the door.

The rest of us were soon retelling the stories of my escapades in Town and I was able to laugh with them. The young men were firm in their assurances that I was no longer the subject of gossip in London, someone else having been only too anxious to take that place with a new *on dit*. Tyler had brought his friends to stay with us for a while but with no particular plans in mind. Their luggage and valets would soon be here in the second carriage. Aunt Cassie went to make the necessary arrangement for their accommodation and I escorted them on a tour of the house and the garden.

* * * * *

Dinner that evening was a happy affair. Tyler had made up with Bessie who now had, in addition, the comfort of Malcolm's presence to restore her. The five young men stayed at table with the port while Bessie, the aunts and I adjourned to the drawing room.

Aunt Penny remarked, "If only there were another young lady or two, you young people might have a pleasant evening of dancing."

"Oh no, we do not need anyone else," I remarked. "I do not mind playing for them."

"But Bertie, I cannot dance with them all!" wailed Bessie.

"Oh. I did not realize what I was saying," I answered in confusion. "Of course, you cannot dance with all five of them. We must just plan to invite someone for another evening. Perhaps we might play whist or —"

I was interrupted by Bessie who squealed and clapped her hands. "We can play charades. We haven't done that in a long time. And there are all those old clothes up in the attic!"

Aunt Penny looked thoughtful for a moment and then said. "But why not have a masquerade party? Invite Squire's family and the Hamdens. You could dress up all of our guests with ease, I think."

Bessie and I looked at each other. Bessie jumped up and threw her arms around Aunt Penny. "That's a famous idea, Aunt Penny. The cir —" She stopped herself and gave me a look I could not understand. "When the men return we can make our plans."

They accepted our plan with eagerness. We each took a candle and proceeded up the three flights of stairs to the attic. With no clear idea of what we should find we tore open the boxes and, holding up one delight after another, laughed with glee.

I found an emerald satin dress with a full skirt and the waistline where it should be. It would be nearly long enough for me after I'd unpicked the stitches holding up the hem. I turned this way and that, holding it up to me and I decided I should wear it whether or not I could think of a suitable game to match it.

A loud clanking came from a far corner and Simon appeared out of the gloom, dressed in the top half of a suit of armor, dragging the lower part on the floor behind him, a feathered helm in his other hand. "I say, shall I be the ghost of someone in this, or should I be Henry V?" he asked as he clanked his way over to me.

Tyler appeared in a long satin coat of a bright pink, wearing a broad-brimmed hat with a matching curled feather jammed on his head over a long curly wig. "Would I make a good Bonnie Prince Charlie, do you think?" He snatched off the hat and made a low sweeping bow. The wig went askew and he peered out at us from between the curls. We all laughed at him.

Bessie cried, "Look at me!" as she pirouetted into our midst. She had removed her gown in the darkness and was now clothed in tightly fitting, brightly colored satin breeches and shirt. A small peaked cap was perched precariously atop her curls. She tapped Malcolm lightly with the riding crop in her hand and said, "Aye, Oi'll be yer jock, m'lud. 'Ow much is me cut, then, if'n Oi takes the cup?" Malcolm flinched at her remarks, then joined in the laughter.

"Don't get any ideas, my love. I intend to do all the racing in this family," he answered her. He had found a tiger skin and draped it across his body then leered at her in such a ferocious manner that she cringed away from him. She dropped down to her knees.

Clasping her hands together in front of her, she looked up at him and pleaded, "Yes my lord. Whatever you say, my lord."

"That's it, Silverton," said Tyler. "Show her who's in charge right from the beginning, or you'll lose out. She can be the most beguiling wench."

He ducked his head to avoid the crop that Bessie threw at him. Even from her kneeling position she was amazingly accurate but the crop only glanced off his head. He caught it as it fell and shook it at her in mock anger. "That's enough of that, my girl." He looked around the dimly lit room and asked, "Where has Harry taken himself off to?"

A banshee wail came just then from the other end of the room. I caught my breath and held it while Bessie quickly rose to her feet and clasped Malcolm's arm. We all looked at each other. The wail came closer and then suddenly died out, followed by Harry's raucous laughter. "Hold up a candle or two, I cannot see my way!" he called. Simon and Tyler held up their candles and peered in the direction of the sound. The wail began again and there was Harry dressed in a kilt and attempting to play the bagpipes that went with it.

"Where is my sword?" called Tyler. "A cavalier should have had a sword. I need one to put this poor thing out of its misery." He pretended to lunge at the bagpipes. Harry backed out of the way, falling over Gareth, who was crawling across the floor toward us under a large bearskin, complete with a snarling-mouthed head.

This was too much for the rest of us and we collapsed in laughter. My sides hurt from too much hilarity. Thank goodness I did not feel the need to wear stays in the country or I should have been ill or have swooned away by this time. As we were now all seated on the floor anyway, we made ourselves even more comfortable with pillows that were thrown around and, by the light of the candles, proceeded to end our evening in pleasant conversation.

* * * * *

We were so engrossed in our conversation that all thought of games flew from our heads. Tyler disappeared at one point but soon returned. A footman came in, struggling manfully with a large tray carrying two pitchers of lemonade and a multitude of jangling glasses. Tyler followed carrying a heaping platter of sugar biscuits. We made short work of the first pitcher as we had stirred up clouds of dust in our rummaging around.

Bessie mentioned the idea of a masquerade party and everyone agreed it was a marvelous idea. We settled on an evening less than a week away and began to make plans. An imaginary guest list soon turned into about twenty-five young people from the surrounding area.

It was amazing to all of us when Harry pulled a watch from his pocket. After carefully inspecting it by the light of the nearest candle, he pronounced the time to be nearly midnight. Sighing regretfully we all got up and trooped downstairs to our beds. The easy camaraderie we had established boded well for the extended presence of the three young men Tyler had brought with him. Malcolm fitted into our family as if he had been born to it. We had even given him a room to use when it became too late of an evening to return to his own home.

Next morning we apprised the aunts of our decision about the party and they assumed the responsibility for it. It seemed only proper that we should all help as we had not had a really large party at Hadleighwoode for some time, but the aunts would not hear of it. It would after all, make good practice for the coming festivities of Bessie's wedding.

And so we passed the next week in a golden glow of lazy days and pleasant evenings. We went on picnics and to see the ruins of a famous nearby Abbey, on pleasant afternoon trips by carriage to nearby neighbors, sometimes spending the evening as well. Invitations to our party were received with great good humor and anticipation.

I fell easily back into the role of Young Miss of the Dower House, even though we were back at the great house. Bessie and the young men spent their allotted time in the stables, or trying out various horses in anticipation of the Derby. I was not looking forward with any happiness to the end of our idyll, the "repairing lease" as Nick had so quaintly put it.

I had tried on several occasions to question Tyler about the giant in the bookstore but he was always too busy just going here or there, or about to do this or that. Gradually the memory faded somewhat and there were so many other things to think about that I just forgot about him. I should probably never see him again anyway. It seemed more important to help with planning our party as I was not of the temperament to be included with the others in their horsy business.

Meanwhile the masquerade party was a smashing success. The house looked lovely and had a fresh fragrance about it that only added to the pleasure. The guests arrived disguised beyond all recognition. The Squire and his family all came and immediately Harry paired off with Tessa. More of Bessie's lightning, no doubt. He could not be faulted on his birth, which was of more importance to the Squire than his wealth. They made a handsome couple and I was happy for them both.

We offered a prize for the best costume and Harry's kilted costume was the unanimous winner, on the condition that he did not attempt to play the bagpipes. Much laughter ensued at this pronouncement, following which I took my place at the pianoforte to play for the dancing.

It was a lovely warm evening and the doors were open to the terrace. Some of the dancers swirled out there. Overall the happy laughter of the guests was like an obbligato to the music. Bessie and Mal were continually stopped and extended happy wishes. It occurred to me that they had not had an engagement party. Tyler and his friends were the object of much admiration from the young ladies and were nearly worn out by dancing with each of them.

Someone mentioned a circus that would be coming to the next village. The very word stirred a faint quivering within me but I resolved not to let it discompose me. I had not seen a circus since the disastrous one of five summers ago, not even the most famous one—Astley's—in London. Sometimes the event did not justify the name, being only a band of traveling Gypsies with their glittery gimcracks, as I remembered only too well. But this one seemed to emphasize their theatrical entertainment, for little was mentioned about a display of any type of animals. It made no difference to me. I would not go.

Tyler and Bessie seemed to be spending more time together but I noticed that on some occasions, whenever I appeared, they would hastily spring apart. I was so happy to be back home that I was oblivious to what I expect a more observant person would have noticed. But I went on my merry way, little expecting what lay in store for me.

I certainly enjoyed the company of Tyler's friends especially as by now they were more by way of being brothers than anything else, which greatly pleased me. For a while I had been concerned that one of them might be in the nature of a suitor, which I did not wish. I was now firmly convinced that I should be happy being a spinster and all the teasing of my extended "family" could not convince me otherwise.

I overheard scraps of conversation now and then, such as "Perfect for her", "Wait until you see him", and "Such a change, truly", but gave them no consideration at all.

Chapter Eight

sɔ

Talk of the circus washed around me. I ignored it, immersed as I was in plans for the engagement party. This was to take place two days after the day the circus was to make its local appearance. Bessie and all the young men were most eager to attend the rustic entertainment. I was determined that I should stay home and help the aunts with all the last-minute details that are so important to the success or failure of such a festivity.

When they had all finally arrived home very late that night they were excited and happy and full of laughter. They tried to convince me that I had missed the best entertainment that had ever come to Kent. Finally, I agreed with them, if only to get them to be quiet and retire for the night. There were still strange little looks being thrown from one to another and interrupted sentences but I was too oblivious to regard them. To my infinite regret.

The next morning, the day before the engagement party, a groom wearing Nick's livery arrived with news that threw everyone into confusion and threatened to overset everything. Nick's message, accompanied by regrets that he could not deliver it in person, was to the effect that he had accepted an offer for my hand in marriage. I nearly swooned as Tyler read this portion of the letter. Bessie rushed to my side and clasped my hands in hers as Tyler silently read the rest of the missive.

"Bertie! That's marvelous news."

"Oh think you so?" I inquired. I was so shaken that I could barely whisper the words. "Nick knows exactly how I feel about that subject, so it is obviously just some prank that he is playing. He'll come home soon and we'll all laugh about it.

Wait and see. This isn't real." I tried laughing to show off my disdain but the very first attempt turned into a sob and I whirled away from them. I rushed up the stairway to my room without listening to the final and most important part of the letter.

When Bessie came into my room a few minutes later she was uneasy in her approach to me. "Are all the plans made for the party?" she asked.

I sat up and brushed the hair away from my face. "Yes."

"Will there be dancing?" Why was she asking this again, I wondered, when she had already asked it of me several times.

"Yes, I'm going to play on the pianoforte Bessie, as I've already informed you."

"Oh yes. That's right. I remember now." She walked over to the dressing table and began to fidget with the items displayed there. "Will there be any other music?"

I frowned at her. "No. Why would there be? I always play for the dancing. Or don't you think I'm good enough anymore?" I couldn't keep a touch of bitterness out of my voice and she turned quickly to face me.

"Oh no Bertie. I never meant that. You know I think you're wonderful. I just meant that, in case you wished to dance, there would be no one to play so that you might. Dance, that is." She was so ill at ease that my suspicions were aroused.

"Bessie, do you know something that I should know but that you are not telling me?"

She turned to me, my dearly beloved twin, who was closer to me than anyone in the world and with her eyes like saucers, replied, "Me?"

"Yes. You are the only other person in this room that I am aware of, not being partial to ghosts. Why are you fidgeting so? Someone must know something and I dearly wish it was me."

"Well," she began and then stopped, shuffling her feet. "Bertie — don't you want to be married?"

"No," I replied. "I've said as much many times since I returned from London. Did you not listen?"

To my astonishment, Bessie then ran to the door and as she flung herself through it, she cried, "I'll talk to you later, Bertie. I've just remembered —" And she was gone. I wished I knew what was happening, or about to happen, or had happened.

* * * * *

"No! This is too much! Never say he is coming here?" I looked around the room in panic. "I don't want to see anyone, most especially him."

A rumble from the doorway caused us all to turn around. A blond giant strolled through the entrance to the room and came over to us, a huge blond dog by his side. My jaw dropped. Where was Millett? How had these two escaped his notice? My thoughts whirled in my head as the giant held out his hand to me. With a snap I closed my mouth and looked up at him. Green eyes sparkled with humor as he smiled at me and I recognized him as the man from the Opera and the bookstore! A mere second later I suddenly realized that this was Sean, my nemesis from the circus five years ago. I wished that the floor would open beneath me and swallow me whole.

Suddenly, the looks flashing from one to another of the younglings or Bessie and the many interrupted sentences made sense to me. I knew that once again I had been the victim of a loving conspiracy. I didn't know what to think about first! Words refused to form in my brain, as I stood there staring at Sean, disbelieving the reality of his having not been killed in the war after all! My mouth opened to say something, then closed with a snap, as I turned helplessly from one to another of my family and then back to Sean. I thought I might swoon again and could feel my knees beginning to weaken, as if they were no longer capable of supporting me, "I —"

Without my realizing it, my hand suddenly found itself in his great paw. He raised it to his lips and a butterfly danced across my knuckles. Somehow he did not seem as much larger than me as I remembered him. For back then, better he had been in the freak show than in the animal cage! Now however, I am six feet tall and he exceeded this by a good six inches. He must have weighed at least fifteen stone but I don't think there was a speck of fat on him. He appeared to be solid muscle, having added breadth to his height in the intervening years. His golden curls—although shorter than previously—still defied the carefully coiffured look so in fashion, tumbling down to meet his collar and surrounding his handsome face, which was now clean-shaven.

Oh yes, he was handsome! He was in truth even more beautiful than I recalled. Dressed in a deep gold-colored velvet coat, his waistcoat was embroidered with gold threads. His unmentionables were a snowy white as were his shirt and cravat and his Hessians were so shiny that I am sure you could have seen your face in them. I was as stunned as if I had been hit over the head by a falling tree. He just stood there looking lazily at me with the smile still in place. Without taking his gaze from my face, he said quietly, "Tyler?"

"Sorry, my lord," Tyler answered. From somewhere deep within me, I thought "my lord?", followed instantly by "no, no, you ninny!" I snatched my hand from his grasp and glared at him.

"Bertie, you remember our friend, Sean Brett, who has become the Earl of Droghlin and—"

I gave him no time to finish. "An Irish—!" I started to say but closed my mouth instead and turned to leave the room. I didn't trust myself not to blurt out my feelings. I needed time to myself to realize—and understand—that my hopes had come true, he was not dead!"

My hand was once again in his paw as he rumbled softly, "Lady Bertie, I am so pleased."

"Well I am not!" I said as I pulled my hand from his and for safekeeping, tucked it behind my back. For even safer keeping, I sent the other one to keep it company. I raised my head and dredging up anger to accompany the words, said, "I would be most pleased were you to leave me—"

Tyler's hand was now over my mouth. He looked at Brett and said, "My apologies, Brett, I had not yet finished my explanation. This hellion here will keep interrupting me." He looked at me, a furious scowl on his face." Bertie, this gentleman is my guest, as well as Nick's and I believe I do still live here as well as you do. I would remind you who you are. I will remove my hand if you will promise to behave." He gave me a little shake and I nodded.

I retreated from them all and looked around me. Simon, Gareth and Harry were also now in the room, as well. I felt ashamed of my outburst. "I beg your pardon, sir. I have not been well. I think I quite lost my head. And now, if you will excuse me..." I managed to take three steps before my hand found itself on his arm. He patted it with his other paw.

"I should be very pleased, Lady Bertie, if you would let me once again extend my most sincere apologies for my behavior of five years ago. I promise you it was not meant to end that way. At the time we planned our famous stunt it seemed great fun. I am most sincerely sorry that you were so embarrassed and frightened." His face showed great concern as he said these pretty words and I felt myself softening somewhat. "Please say that you can forgive me for my thoughtlessness, Lady Bertie?"

I seemed to be two persons inside myself. One wanted very much to say yes but the other was still filled with anger and confusion. Somewhere in the middle there might be yet a third self, who could contend with both these thoughts. In the meantime, the hand that he was still holding was shivering with ever-stronger tingles. They were now running up my arm so strongly that in spite of myself I glanced at my arm to see if the tremors were visible to everyone. To my immense relief my arm appeared to be normal. I looked around at the faces of the others and was surprised to see looks of hopeful anticipation. I was so hopelessly outnumbered it seemed I might as well concede.

"I might be able to do so, my lord, if you will but answer a few more questions for me?" I looked up at him and was so dazzled by his smile that my knees began to wobble beneath my skirts.

"Thank you. I will do my best." Now he looked around at the others, then at the doors leading to the terrace. "It is a perfectly lovely day, is it not? Perhaps you might walk with me, as I explain?"

I could see no great harm in this as we should be in sight of the others as we strolled. I looked at Tyler, who nodded. Brett and I started for the doors.

"Bertie," Tyler called. "I never finished." He subsided as Brett shook his head at him. Tyler shrugged his shoulders and turned away from us.

Brett opened the doors and we went out into the glorious morning. I looked up at him and said, "And now my lord, you were going to answer my questions."

"Did you know I was at school with Jonathon? He always told me about you and advised me to just wait it out," he said.

I once again removed my hand from his grasp and asked, "But what has that to do with why you're here now?"

"Spoke to Nick about you, asked for permission," he said. What on earth was he talking about?

I looked anxiously back at the house. Why had Tyler let me walk out here like this? If I screamed, would they be able to get here fast enough?

"What are you talking about? Permission to do whatever it is you did five years ago?" I asked in some confusion.

He walked over to a nearby rose and after cutting the yellow blossom, carefully detached the thorns before he turned back and presented it to me with a bow. I was stunned.

"Thank you," I murmured.

"Nothing at all, I assure you. Were it my garden I'd cut them all and give them to you." He looked sad at the thought, then brightened. "Send some, that's what I'll do," he said, nodding.

Taking a firm grip on myself, I said, "My lord, how did you... Ah, five years ago, that is... How did you make the fur, that is...it was so...it fit you so..." I came to a stop, unable to put into words what it was that I wanted to know.

Thunder rumbled nearby. No, it was just Sean laughing. "Oh that was Lady Bessie. She made a glue of flour and water and pasted little bits of fur all over me, whatever we could find."

My face reddened down to my waist, as I squeaked, "Bessie? All over?"

"Well no, just where there was no place to sew it on, do you see."

I had a sudden remembrance and turned to accuse him. "You winked at me!"

"Yes, certainly I did. You were so close. I could not resist."

The blond animal had accompanied us into the garden and was now busily licking my hand. "And this...this?"

This was leaning heavily into me, pushing me closer to Brett. I leaned back.

"Down, sir!" said the giant and the creature immediately dropped to the ground. "Mind your manners and present yourself!" It sat up and extended a front limb to me, its tongue lolling out of its great mouth.

"Oh," I exclaimed. "Do you say that this is a dog?"

"What did you think he was?"

"I...I did not know, for a certainty." I laughed to cover my embarrassment. "Perhaps it could be a pony?"

The thunder rumbled again. "I was sure you would remember Blondel."

"Blondel?" I echoed. "Never say that this, this huge animal is Blondel?"

"Yes. He was just a pup five years ago and hadn't yet got his growth. Blondel is an Irish wolfhound. His full name is Brett's Blondel. Raise 'em, you know." He seemed inordinately pleased with himself.

"Do they all get to be so, er, large?" I asked.

"The, ah, gentleman dogs mostly do. The ladies remain somewhat smaller."

I shuddered. The shoulders of this animal came up to my waist. When he stood near Brett, his head made a convenient resting place for his owner's hand. "Do you have many of them?" I asked.

Brett looked at me in confusion. "Of course. Said I raise 'em."

"Why do you call him Brett's Blondel? Why Blondel at all?"

"My name's Brett. Tradition has it so. All the names start with 'B'. This fellow has brothers named Bolingbroke, Burghley, Beowulf, Bothwell."

"No...ah, sisters?"

"They are Boadicea and Boleyn."

"Are they all named for history, then?" I asked.

"No. Each batch of names comes from a different source. The military litter was Brevet, Brigadier, Bullet, Bosun, Bravo and Brittania." He was lost in thought. "Then there was the botanical bunch—Butterfly, Bamboo, Bluebell, Basket, Bramble and Blossom."

"Do you never run out of names, my lord?" In spite of myself I was intrigued and interested.

"No, although it is sometimes a little chancy, depending on the proportion of, ah, brothers to sisters."

"And they are always all called by a name that starts with 'B'?"

"There is one exception. Each d—er, the first litter after the new heir takes over, has the first, ah, gentleman dog named for the king that granted us the title."

I could think of no king whose name started with a "B". "And who was that?" I asked.

"Richard III, when he was Lord Lieutenant of Ireland, knighted a Brett for gallantry. Ever since, one pup is called 'Dickon'."

"Not the monster?" I cried.

"You should not say such things, Lady Bertie. He was a good man and someday history will prove it. He had no hump and was not twisted...in any way. The Bretts consider it an honor to have received the title from him and to name the pup for him. The first 'Dickon' was a present to him when he stayed at my home, once." His voice, which had been soft and gentle, rose in volume as he became enthused on the subject and I flinched away from him.

"Pardon, Lady Bertie. I did not mean to speak so." He had the grace to look slightly embarrassed. "Forget myself sometimes. Promised Nick I wouldn't frighten you and just look at me. Try not to do it again."

He smiled at me, then dropped to one knee, one hand thrown across his chest, the other to his head, palm out. I couldn't help it, I laughed. "Say you'll forgive me," he pleaded.

I could hardly speak for laughing. "Get up, you great lummox. What will the others think—?" My voice died away at the frosty look on his face.

With easy grace he rose to his feet. The frosty look was replaced by a smile, complete with a devilish glint in his eyes.

"Why that's easy, Lady Bertie. They'll think you owe me a forfeit."

"A forfeit?" Hastily I backed away from him.

He stood there looking at me. I swear I could see the thought of what I both longed for, as well as dreaded the most, as it appeared in his head.

"Yes, just a little one. I think, ah—yes, I will have a kiss."

I turned to run from him but he caught me up to him. Where in the world was everyone when I needed them? I pounded his chest and hissed with shock as my hand hit a stone wall.

Looking up at him, I whispered, "But I don't wish to be kissed. I don't like it."

"You don't?" he asked, softly. "Ah, but I do, very much." He placed one great paw to either side of my face and gently lowered his lips to mine. My eyes crossed as I watched his face get closer and closer. I stiffened myself in anger, remembering the wet, hasty kisses that had been pressed on me by young men at our neighborhood affairs. This was nothing like. Nothing.

His lips were like butterflies, dancing lightly, resting gently, then dancing again. One of his hands was encircling my back, drawing me close. To my dismay, my hands crept up and were wrapping themselves around his great neck. I could not breathe. Time stood still. Why had no one ever told me about this? How different a man feels when he isn't your brother!

Abruptly, I found myself standing apart from him, gasping for air. I looked up to see a grin on his face. I tried to speak but found myself too furious for words.

He said, "I was right, don't you think?"

Words came tumbling from my mouth. "No I don't. You great bumbling looby! You do belong in a cage." And with those words I drew back my arm and gave him a great whack across his cheek.

His eyes blazed and the thunder began again.

Tears blurred my vision as I ran across the garden and came hard up against Tyler.

"What have you done now, you silly girl?" my darling brother asked.

Isn't that just like a man? I had been insulted and assaulted, made to look like a fool and his concern was for his friend. His male friend. Tyler shook me, bringing me back to the scene. "This, this feather-wit you call friend. I never want…" I turned to face Brett.

"I have some new names for your next animals, sir. Have you never thought of Beast, Barbarian, Bothersome, Bungle, Bully." I gasped for air. "How about Borgia or Bonaparte?" I pushed Tyler out of my way but he grabbed my arm and pulled me back again.

"Bertie, Bertie, you do not know what you are saying. Or who you're saying it to. Hush. I tried to tell you before but you kept barging in. Bertie, Brett is, in addition to being the Earl of Droghlin, the—"

"I don't care," I cried. I kicked him. "Let me go!"

"Not until you apologize to His Grace."

"His Grace?" I mumbled, shocked at the fury in Tyler's voice.

"Yes, through a quirk of fate, Brett is now also the Duke of Kilnarne. To think that he should be so insulted in our home. What would Nick say?"

What would everyone say? I was mortified. To stand in my garden screaming like a banshee at the Earl of Droghlin would have been bad enough but to do it to the Duke of Kilnarne no doubt placed me entirely beyond the pale! Great heavens! No matter the provocation, it just wasn't done. Well almost. I solved that problem at least for the present. This time I really did swoon.

Chapter Nine

❦

My cheeks were tingling as I opened my eyes. Bessie's hand was halfway to my face in another attempt to slap it but I clutched at it and said, "Not necessary!"

She looked at me with a puzzled look on her face. "Whatever did you do, Bertie? I have never seen Tyler so angry. He came in here carrying you in his arms and — well, he just threw you on the sofa. He stomped out and said to call him when you woke up." She started to get to her feet but I grasped her hand and closed my eyes again.

"Are you hurt, Bertie?" she asked.

"No but I wish I might be dead," I groaned.

"Tell me about it?"

"I'm not sure I know it all myself." A sudden thought penetrated my foggy state and I sat up. "Bessie, why didn't you ever tell me that you fixed that animal costume for Brett?"

She lowered her eyes from mine. "There never was a good time," she whispered, as she grasped my hands in hers. "I wanted to, Bertie, so many times but it just never seemed an appropriate moment. I'm so sorry. I swear I never knew how you felt about him. When you were preparing to go to London earlier this year, I found your journal, remember? That's when I realized that you had had a tendre for him, I wanted to just die. I was so ashamed, Bertie."

"Did you know he had become a duke?"

"Yes," she whispered. "I learned that only yesterday. It seems the late duke was his second cousin and Sean, as the nearest blood relative, has inherited the title and all that goes with it."

I groaned again covering my face with my hands. "Why ever didn't you tell me?"

"When was there the opportunity?" she asked. "I only found out at the circus and he arrived here today." Bessie pulled my hands down and looked up into my face, a look of horror starting to replace the one of concern that had been there. "Never say — oh Bertie, what have you done?"

In a very small voice I answered her. "I called him a great bumbling looby and slapped his face — hard." As I remembered the scene in the garden I began to shiver. "And, er, I said some other things too, probably not the type of things one should say to a duke."

Her eyes were round in astonishment. "You slapped his face? Why — ?"

"He kissed me." The memory of that brought the red to my face and I looked for something with which to fan myself.

"I don't see— What is so wrong about kissing your betrothed? Mal and I do it all the time. I find it quite enjoyable."

"Betrothed?" I croaked at her. "Are you being more of a widgeon than usual? I am betrothed to no one, nor do I intend to be and so I shall tell Nick."

"Oh Bertie. You still don't know, do you?"

"Know what?" I asked as my stomach sank to my feet. I had the horrible premonition that I did know. And I desperately wished that I didn't. I looked at Bessie and waited to hear her confirm my feelings of doom.

"When Tyler read Nick's message this morning, Nick said that he had accepted an offer for your hand in marriage. Remember?"

How could I forget? I said nothing.

"You left the room before finding out who had asked for you."

In a dead voice, I responded, "And that someone is Sean? Sean, who is now a duke?"

"Yes," Bessie replied. "We were so pleased for you."

"The world has lost its wits indeed!" I moaned to myself. "So pleased that no one thought to tell me? Why has no one bothered to even ask me?" I cried. "I cannot believe this!" I was torn between again collapsing on the sofa or going out to do battle.

"Bertie, listen to me. We all love you, you know that. Every woman must marry and Brett seemed to be all that was wonderful. He is so large and charming and funny and he is a duke! Of course Nick said yes. He would not be doing his best for you were he to have said otherwise." She reached over and wiped a tear from my eye with a scrap of lace that she considered to be a handkerchief. "My dear, you will be happy, I know you will." That was too much for me. I jumped up from the sofa.

"Bessie, I have become extremely shackle-shy and you know it very well. It is true that I did want to go to London for a Season but I soon discovered that idea to have been a great mistake. I did not suit at all and I really only wanted to come back home. I suit only Hadleighwoode and Hadleighwoode suits me. I love being an aunt and looked forward to nothing more than always being 'Aunt Bertie'." I stood up and paced the floor angrily. I reminded myself quite of Joan— "Aha! It was Joan, wasn't it? Joan wreaking her revenge on me."

"No Bertie. Joan had nothing to do with it. Nick, Jon and Tyler were the only ones involved. It is a wonderful match for you. Just think, you'll be a duchess."

"I don't want to be a duchess", I wailed. "It is quite the worst thing I can imagine. I begin to think he *is* a bumble-witted looby. Bessie, I think you have all gone mad!"

Tyler came into the room. "Ah, you are yourself again." He came over and stood in front of me. "Whatever possessed you to—?"

"Me? You will never convince me that I have done anything wrong. If you had seen fit to tell me that that great oaf was a duke—"

Tyler grabbed my hand and twisting it up behind my back drew me close to him. He glared at me. It was difficult to see him clearly, we were standing so close to each other. "Any gentleman of our acquaintance who enters our home is entitled to be treated with courtesy and respect, Bertie. Brett is a duke, although a singularly un-arrogant one, as you should remember from the times that he has spent visiting here but that should not affect your behavior. You will apologize to him, Bertie," he said as he shook me a little for emphasis.

I glared back at him. "And in my own home am I not also entitled to be treated with courtesy and respect?"

"Bertie, he was treating you with courtesy and respect. All he did was kiss you which I don't think calls for such behavior from you. You must apologize to him."

"Tyler," I said in a small voice. "I do not know if I can face him again. Could I not write him a little note, instead?"

"No. But to make it easier for you and to still whatever talk there may be, we can invite him to join us for our social gathering tonight. With other people about you will not have to see that much of him."

Bessie clapped her hands and jumped up. "A party! Just the thing! We shall be able to dance—"

Tyler released my arm. I rubbed it to take away the pins and needles that had invaded it. I looked at him in bewilderment. "Do you mean for me to apologize to him in front of the entire company then?"

"No, no, of course not. But it should be fairly easy for you to find a quiet time apart from the others to do your pretty to him." Finally, he smiled at me. "That should not be so hard, should it?"

I mumbled something unintelligible. Taking it for assent, he patted my shoulder. "Well then, that's taken care of." He walked to the doorway.

"Where is His Grace?" I asked quietly.

"He's gone back to the inn where he is staying. He said he had something there that he wanted to bring you."

"Oh no." Was it possible to feel even more wretched than I was already?" Did he say what it was?"

"No, just a present for you." Tyler was already on his way out of the room.

"Tyler!" I called. "If this present is in any way connected to this supposed betrothal I shall not answer for my conduct I do assure you."

"Bertie, do not worry about that now. One step at a time, please. First you must apologize to him. We can worry about the betrothal later."

"Why did you never think to tell me about this supposed betrothal?" I asked.

"I don't know," he answered. "I thought you would be pleased with it. Not every country miss can snare a duke her first night out in society." His rich laugh followed him out the door. I turned to Bessie in bewilderment.

"Is this entire family moonstruck?" I asked. She had no answer, just gave me a small sickly smile.

* * * * *

To have a nap suddenly seemed to be the thing most desired so I trudged up to my room. My brain was so full of bewilderment there was no room for anything else to be there too.

Before I knew what was happening, Aunt Cassie was shaking me awake. I found myself surrounded by both the aunts and Bessie. It was more attention than I needed or wanted and I shooed the aunts away. Bessie was standing in front of the clothespress picking through my gowns, frowning as she considered each one. With a little exclamation, she pulled one out.

"This is exactly the thing, Bertie," she said, holding it up in front of her. I could not help but laugh at the extra foot of material draped in front of her on the floor. It was a deep gold-colored muslin, with paler ribbons hanging from the misplaced waist and a row of gold embroidery around the hem. The square neckline had a narrower row of the same embroidery around it and the little sleeves were tied with a bow to match the ribbons. "You can wear Brett's roses in your hair," she said.

"What roses? Now what has he done?" I sighed.

"He sent you a small bouquet of the most lovely yellow roses. One or two of them in your hair, or perhaps on your wrist—"

"Or perhaps I should wear the entire bunch, vase and all?" I inquired.

In all seriousness, she answered, "No, I think just one or two of them."

I shook my head. I took the dress from her hand, threw it on the bed and taking her by the hand, led her to the bed, sat her down, then sat beside her. "Bessie, why is it that no one hears what I say? Does no one believe me? Please listen carefully. I—do—not—in—tend—to—mar—ry—Brett. Is that clear enough? I do not wish to hear any more about this subject."

"But Bertie," she interrupted. "He's in love with you."

"Fustian!" I shouted at her. "He could not possibly be in love with me. Even if he was, it doesn't matter, because I am not in love with him." If I told myself that often enough, I should be able to believe it. I must have been very loud in my exhortation, because Aunt Cassie came bustling through the door to my room.

"Hush Bertie, everyone in the house can hear you."

"I don't care, Aunt Cassie. And at any rate, it does not matter because no one hears me or listens to what I say. I might as well talk to the wall."

"Calm yourself, my dear. No one will take you to the altar in chains, you know."

"Maybe not but how many days or weeks on bread and water shall I have?"

"Bertie! Bertie. Can you really believe that of your family?" Aunt Cassie was disturbed at the thought. "We only want what is best for you and what you want, if it can be done. If this nice young man is not it, then we'll not say any more about it. But you must give him a chance. Nick has given him permission to talk to you. He would not have done that without great consideration, you know."

I looked from her to Bessie, not at all liking what I saw on their faces. Turning away I slowly walked to the nearest wall. I began to bang my head against it. Realizing the futility of my actions, I rested my forehead against the coolness. I heard the door close and looked around to see who had left. It was Aunt Cassie.

"Bertie, do you really mean that you will not have him?" Bessie asked in a quiet voice. "You are very sure?"

"Yes, yes, yes and yes. Can it be that you are finally beginning to listen to what I say?" I asked.

"If you are really sure, then I shall help you in whatever way I may. And Mal will too, I know. We both know what it should be and if it is not that way for you, then you will not be pushed into anything you don't want. I promise you." She meant her words, I knew, which gave me some reason to be hopeful.

Dinner that evening was just the family, Mal and the younglings. We didn't linger over it as there were still things to be done before the socializing could begin. There were great bowls of fresh flowers and extra branches of candles in all the rooms. The smell of lemon and beeswax hovered lightly, indicating the hard work of the maids. The doors to the terrace were all open and occasionally a gentle breeze wafted through. Tyler came over to me and taking my hand led me out-of-doors. He swallowed and said, "Bertie, I am truly sorry that this has happened in just this way. Kilnarne is a wonderful friend and no brother could hope for more for his little sister than he can offer. I think I would give ten years of my life if we had not played that joke and overset you so badly."

I smiled and said, "He was a strangely attractive beast, I give you that." My wayward mind insisted on remembering just how attractive he had been with all that golden skin showing through the bits of fur. "I could not imagine how his fur was all bits and pieces of colors and patterns and it was that which took me too close to the cage. I am sorry too."

He patted my hand and looking off into the distance, asked, "Will you be able to apologize to him and not lose your temper again?"

"I still think it would be better if I could just write him a note."

"You forget that he is bringing you a present. No—" he lifted his hand to silence me, "it is not what you may be thinking. I do believe you will quite like it."

"I should like it best if he would not do it at all, Tyler."

"Bertie, Brett is a friend and a gentleman. I would ask you to remember that. You do not have to do more than make your apology and gracefully accept his gift. Then you may do as you wish." He turned and looked at me. Placing a finger under my chin he lifted my head so that I had to look at his face. His eyes pleaded with me but he made no sound. I sighed.

"I promise I will try my best. Can you—?" I stopped. I knew my face was turning red. "Tyler," I whispered.

"Yes love. What is it?" he whispered back.

"I, er, don't…ah, wish for him to kiss me again. Please?" I looked at him but this time the pleading was in my eyes.

"Oh." I thought I could see the corners of his mouth beginning to turn up but at the look on my face he controlled it. "I will try, Bertie. I will try."

"Thank you" I whispered and went back into the drawing room.

* * * * *

I hoped to escape the dancing by offering to play the pianoforte and for a while my plan was successful. I was looking through the music for something suitable to accompany a quadrille, when there was a sudden hush in the room. I turned around to see what had happened and there was Brett—or Kilnarne as I supposed I ought to think of him now—in the doorway, an amiable smile on his face.

When he saw me he came straight for me, nodding and smiling at those he passed, although he spoke to no one. As he reached the pianoforte, he bowed and held out his hand to me. I felt like I am sure the fox must feel when cornered by the hounds. I could not find the air I needed to breathe. Summoning all the courage I could find, I smiled tentatively at him and offered my hand. As he gracefully bent to brush it with his lips, the entire room breathed at once and the hiss startled me. He didn't release my hand but exerted a slight pressure on it and I found myself standing in front of him.

"Lady Bertie, you are in very fine looks tonight. I am so pleased to see you." He looked around at the occupants of the room, who were all watching us. He smiled at them all, then turned to me. "Would you be kind enough to honor me with the next dance?"

"Your Grace, I am the music for the dance, so I regret that I must—"

He frowned in my direction. "There is no one else to play?"

"No. It is my custom to provide the music at our little dances, Your Grace." I forced myself to smile at him. "So you see, I do not dance."

"Do you dance if there is other music, Lady Bertie?"

"I prefer to provide the music, Your Grace."

I turned to sit back down but he took my hand again. "Do you take a rest from your playing? I feel that your hands and arms must deserve a rest at times."

"At times, Your Grace." I looked around the room at all the faces staring at us. I could feel my face beginning to turn red. "I think that I should resume the music and encourage our guests to do something other than stare at us."

He released my hand and walked over to the chairs along the edge of the room. To my surprise, he picked one up and carried it over to where I was sitting and placed it beside me. "I shall turn the pages of your music for you." I was in a panic. How could I get rid of him? I could not sit for any length of time with him so close to me without getting into further difficulties. My fingers would turn to mush and I should not be able to produce any comprehensible music at all.

"I do not use the music very much, my lord. Won't you please join our guests in dancing?" I was busily sorting through the music as I said these words and, also, I discovered, holding my breath waiting for his answer.

"No, no, I am very content to just sit here by your side for a while. Will it be long before this set of dances is over?" He settled himself more comfortably on the chair as he said this and at the same time threw me a charming smile. I hoped the chair wouldn't break landing him on the floor.

"I was just looking for a quadrille when you came in. After that, we always stop for a bit as everyone then needs refreshment." He was so close that I could smell his clean, fresh scent. How I wished he would just go away but of course, he would not until I had apologized. My fingers stumbled over the keys as I began to play. I nodded to indicate when it was time to turn the page. As he leaned across in front of me I thought I must surely swoon again, if he were to be so close very often. He was so very large that even in such a large room I felt smothered by him.

I could not seem to concentrate on the music and the swirling dancers were making me dizzy. My fingers faltered and he was instantly all concern. "Perhaps you might like some fresh air, Miss Bertie?" he asked. "Or maybe a glass of lemonade?" What I really wanted was for him to just go away but that didn't appear to be a possibility.

Finally the dance came to an end and I wiped my damp fingers on my handkerchief. He inquired of me once again, "Air or lemonade, Lady Bertie?"

"I think some air, Your Grace." He took my hand and, as if by magic, our guests parted to make a path for us. "Do you think you might wish for a shawl?" he asked as I shivered.

"No thank you, I am fine," I answered.

He placed my hand on his arm and escorted me to the terrace and my certain doom. Once we were away from any listeners I stopped. Without looking up at him, I murmured, "Your Grace, I am sorry for the things I said to you this morning. Even with such provocation I should not have let my tongue run away with itself." I was amazed that I had managed to get all these words out without stammering and tried to free my hand.

He only tightened his grip and smiled at me. "I think I must apologize to you as well." I was startled by this admission and looked up at him. "Not for the, er, provocation, mind," my mouth dropped open but he continued, "that was as I knew it would be but—ah, for the prank and, er, for not taking the time to court you in a more suitable fashion." He stopped and touched my cheek lightly with one finger, then gently placed that finger under my jaw and closed my still gaping mouth. The surprise made me flinch.

"Always have been one to rush my fences but you see, Lady Bertie, we Bretts always decide things quickly. I knew the moment I saw you that night that I would have no other for my duchess."

"Please, Your Grace, do not—" He gently placed his finger on my lips.

"Please call me Brett. Or would you prefer Sean? Or Kilnarne? Or Droghlin? I have other names if you wish but I do not like to hear you say 'Your Grace'." The easy smile never left his face.

"Other names your, er, ah, Brett?"

"You may remember that my complete name is Sean Conner Carruthers Brett. You may call me whichever of them you choose." He looked down at me with a lover's smile on his face. "I love your name. Zenobia." He rolled the syllables around, stretching the name out. "I knew when I first heard it that you'd be mine. A noble name is Zenobia, don't you think? Marvelous name for a duchess." And, caressing my hand with his, he started walking again. I followed, unwillingly, my head in a whirl. He was imperturbable.

"Zenobia," he said again, softly. "Do you have other names too?" he asked but before I could answer, he made an exclamation which startled me.

"Ah, there it is."

I looked up and saw a footman in strange livery struggling to carry a heavy basket around the corner. "That's good, right there, Mullins," Brett called and tugged me over with him to inspect the basket more closely.

"I brought you a very special gift. You'll like it, I know," he said as he leaned to the basket. He then changed his mind again and steered me to a nearby bench.

Once when Bessie and I were about ten, we came upon an almost-empty decanter of brandy leftover from a gathering of Nick and his friends. It was just sitting there on a table. Feeling very bold, we shared the contents. In a very few moments after we had hastily imbibed some water to wash away the horrible taste, our heads became fuzzy. We staggered around and our speech became slurred. Eventually we became sick. That feeling of queasiness was exactly what I was now feeling. My head was whirling like the tops we used to play with in the nursery and in truth, I was happy to be seated. I did not know if I could have remained standing.

"The motto of the Bretts is 'Steadfast Always', Lady Bertie." He was very serious. "We have always married only for love. Even our women have always married for love."

What was he talking about? His thumb was caressing the back of my hand as he said these words, lulling me into a feeling of lassitude. He had the most disconcerting habit of always looking straight into one's eyes and I felt myself falling under his spell. Never taking his gaze from mine, he gently raised my hand to his lips. But this time he turned it over and the butterflies danced again but this time they skittered across my palm. I shuddered and jerked my hand away as if it had been kissed by a candle. He promptly pulled it back into his clasp and his thumb went to work again. What was this?

"I told you that the first Brett was knighted by Richard III. He was called to fight at Bosworth but his lady was near her confinement and wished him to stay. Richard gave him leave and thus he avoided certain execution, either on the battlefield or for treason." His eyes still held mine.

"Oh," I said, thoroughly confused by both his actions and his words.

"Paid a whopping fine to greedy Henry but kept his head. Since that time, we have always held more to wife than king. No doubt that's why we still have Castle Kilnarne."

"I see," I murmured. But I didn't see. Anything! Why was he telling me all of this?

"I do love you, Lady Bertie. I've loved you for years." His head was coming closer to mine. I drew back. "I knew I must have you. That's why I spoke to Nick."

I jumped up from the bench struggling to keep my temper and my tears where they belonged. "But no one spoke to me, your, er, ah. It could have saved us all much agony if only they had. I do not wish to marry. I do not love you."

"You will," he said as he grasped my flailing hand and pulled me down beside him on the bench. "I told you. Bretts are steadfast and once they see what they want they will have it." That infuriating smile was still in place and directed fully at me.

"And has no woman ever refused?"

He was incredulous at my question. "Of course not. Why ever should they?" he asked.

"I do not wish to marry and I do not love you," I protested, again.

"It may take a while. Told you I rush my fences but you'll like Kilnarne. When you—"

"No!" I shouted. "Your Grace, you have ears, I can see them there on your head. Do you ever use them to listen with?" I was beginning to panic. "I do not plan to see Castle Kilnarne, or anywhere for that matter. I plan to spend the remainder of my life right here at Hadleighwoode, unwed."

"We can spend some time here, if you wish but—"

"No!" I cried. I jerked my hand away from his and pinched myself viciously on the other arm. If only I could awaken from this nightmare!

A noise from the direction of the basket distracted him momentarily. I seized the opportunity and began to run back to the house.

In two steps I had been captured again. "Forgot your present, nearly. Come," he said as we started in that direction. I dug in my heels.

"Please, Your Grace, Brett, whatever you wish to be called—"

"I always favored dearling or sweeting, myself," he interrupted, a grin on his face.

I stamped my foot in fury. I didn't think fast enough to stamp his foot. It was certainly large enough to provide an excellent target. "Your Grace, I am most sincerely aware of the great honor you do me but I can not accept."

"Of course you can."

"I am not well enough born to be a duchess!" I shouted at him.

He looked at me in disgust. "What has that to do with anything? If I think you'll do, you'll do. That's that." The disgust changed to a smile, "And I know you'll do. A fiery duchess! Marvelous!" He continued toward the basket which was now wobbling back and forth on the ground where the footman had placed it. In spite of myself, I was intrigued and drew closer to it.

"Chose this for you myself. Had to go home before I came here and knew it was just the thing." He reached down and pulled the lid off the basket. He came up with a ball of golden fur, which, on closer inspection proved to be a wriggling blonde puppy. Who can resist such an object? I couldn't.

Carefully he set the little animal on the grass, where it staggered, then ran over to my feet and promptly curled up on them. I was too startled to speak. I looked first at the pup and then at Brett. I did not want to smile but couldn't help myself.

"Is it from Blondel?" I asked.

"Blondel is her father," he answered.

"Does she have a name yet?" I reached down to pat the little creature on its head.

"Didn't I tell you I chose her for you myself? Her name is Brett's Beloved!"

"Oh no!" I tried to extricate myself from the position of footrest. "How could you do such a thing?" Finally, I managed to get free and turned to go back to the drawing room.

"Wait!" he cried. "Don't you want her?"

"Not with that name, I don't. Thank you, my lord but no." A step at a time I was retreating.

His face lit up with a sudden smile. "Forgot. You never told me your other names."

I stopped just before the doorway and looked up at him.

"Grace, Your Grace," I began, as I inched my way closer to security. I had not noticed, however, that Blondel, ever faithful, had followed his master to the terrace. As nothing was happening that needed his assistance he had lain down for a nap and was now snoozing peacefully across the door sill. As I turned, I evidently stepped on one of his great feet. He jumped up with a yip just as I turned to go through the door. I never even saw him lying there but as I fell over him, sprawling full length on the floor, I finished my sentence. "Grace is my middle name."

Chapter Ten

ର

My head hurt. That realization was the first I had that something was not quite as it should be. I tried to lift my hand to rub it and I could not move my arm. I tried to open my eyes but it made no difference. Wherever I was, it was so dark that I could not tell if I had succeeded in opening them or not. I must have made a noise because there was a cooling cloth placed on my forehead with the admonition to "Hush".

Again, later, I tried to open my eyes. This time there was light in the room but the pain in my head caused me to hurriedly close them again.

"Close the draperies a little more," someone said.

Another voice said, "Is she coming around, then?"

Someone else groaned. I realized it was me. I felt something soft and warm on my cheek, followed by the cool cloth on my forehead again. I tried to move but found I could not. I turned my head only to wish I had not, as the pain thrust again. Tears made their slow way out of my eyes and welled over and down the side of my face.

I felt my hand being caressed gently and a soothing voice said, "Rest easy, Bertie. You'll be better soon." I was too tired to care and drifted away again.

When next I tried to open my eyes it was again dark but the pain was not as strong. I sensed shapes around me and finally was able to distinguish people. My eyes raised and discovered the familiar canopy over my bed. What were all these people doing in my bedchamber? I tried to sit up but the pain brought me back down again. I felt as though I were tied to the bed. Why was this?

The pain caused by the movement subsided and I lay still for a moment trying to remember what had happened. My mind was a blank except for the pain. Again I felt that wonderful cool cloth on my face and opened my mouth to thank whomever was responsible. I was startled when a croak emerged instead of words.

"Hush, love," a familiar voice said. I couldn't quite place it. "You've been rather ill but you will be fine. Don't try to move." Of course I promptly tried to do just that but was unable to make any of my body respond. I seemed to have all the stability of a bowl of soup. That thought caused my stomach to rumble and I thought how wonderful a bowl of soup would taste right now. I tried to open my mouth to ask for one but instead was pleased by something cool and wet that trickled into it. With difficulty I swallowed and opened my mouth again for more.

I heard several muffled cheers and a wrenching sob saying, "Thank God!" followed by the sound of someone crying. Was that me? After several more swallows of the cool liquid, I tried again to open my eyes and finally succeeded.

Nick was sitting on a chair beside my bed looking more worried than I had ever seen him. Next to him was Aunt Cassie. This time I tried to move only my eyes instead of my head and discovered with no little degree of pleasure that I was able to do this with no pain. It was thus I noticed that there on the other side of the bed was Aunt Penny holding a bowl and a small piece of cloth. Next to her were Tyler, Bessie and Mal. At the foot of the bed, by himself as if in a place of honor, was His Grace, the Duke of Kilnarne. I groaned and closed my eyes.

"Bertie, can you hear me?" asked Nick in a soft voice.

I nodded and winced. Why couldn't I move my arm?

"Bertie, do you know where you are?" Nick asked again.

"Yes," I whispered.

"Do you know what happened to you?"

I tried to think but could not. I opened my eyes and saw Brett. "No," I said, as I closed them again. "No," I repeated.

Nick took my hand and said, "Try to sleep again, my dear. Next time it may be easier." They all disappeared, or maybe I did.

I opened my eyes and it was neither light nor dark. Cautiously I tried to move my head and was pleased that the pain did not discourage me. It was now just a dull ache. My arm would still not move and I frowned at it. I opened my mouth and emitted another croak. Immediately, the cool cloth was again on my forehead. I had never felt anything more wonderful. I turned my head in the other direction, slowly and there was Bessie, tears rolling down her face.

"Bertie? Bertie?" she whispered. "Can you hear me?" I nodded ever-so slightly. "Does your head still hurt so?" she asked tenderly.

Again I nodded and opened my mouth hoping for some more of whatever had been so refreshing. She looked at me with a frown and said, "I don't know what to do. Let me just go get the others."

"No," I mouthed. "Drink."

With a spoon she fed me small amounts of the cool liquid and I rejoiced in the taste. After several swallows, I said, "Tell."

"Do you remember anything?" she asked. My eyes immediately went to the foot of the bed but he wasn't there and a feeling of relief swept over me.

"Do you want Brett?" she asked.

"No!" I croaked a little louder than before.

"Oh," she looked at me in confusion.

"Tell," I said again. "Arm?"

"You broke it when you fell over Blondel. And hit your head. We were all so worried abut you. Brett—"

"When?" I interrupted her.

"Three nights ago at our party," she answered.

I groaned again as memories came flooding back. "Brett?" I asked.

"He's downstairs. Do you want him?"

"No!" I was getting a little stronger.

"He left your side only long enough to go to London to get a famous doctor to tend your arm. They say he set a record for riding from here to there and back again," she enthused.

I tried to move one of my feet and discovered there was a large rock in the middle of the bed. As I prodded it, it moved and made a snuffling noise. "What?" I asked.

Bessie giggled and replied, "That's your Beloved." I groaned again.

"Why?"

"She wouldn't leave you. Brett trained her to be yours and when we tried to keep her out of your room, she howled and cried so much she near drove us all to Bedlam. She's perfectly well behaved and quiet as long as she's near you."

I closed my eyes in frustration and dropped into sleep again.

The next time I was able to open my eyes without a struggle. When I tried to turn my head I discovered that I was able to do so quite easily and with almost no pain. I tried to sit up and discovered that I could not move my arm, as it was encased in bandages with boards tied to it. I frowned down at it and groaned. An answering little whuffle came from the blond lump at the foot of the bed.

"Bertie, my love, you are awake!" Aunt Penny bustled over from the chair by the window. "Are you feeling better, dear?" she asked as she wiped my forehead with the cool cloth.

I tried my voice and found that it worked. "Yes I think so. I am so thirsty, Aunt Penny."

Carefully she lifted my head and helped me to drink from a glass of lemonade.

"Where ?"

"They're all downstairs waiting to see you. Shall I call them?" she asked.

"No. Please. Tell me what happened," I pleaded.

Beloved started inching her way up to the head of the bed, making happy little noises. I frowned at her. Her tail wagged striking limply at my body. She crawled up to my good hand, snuggled her head under it and emitted a happy little sigh. My hand started to caress her soft fur and I couldn't seem to make it stop.

"Beloved has been your most faithful companion, Bertie," Aunt Penny said. "She has been unwilling to leave your bed except for very short walks. I think you have acquired a dog."

"I don't want her, "I answered, as I tried to make my hand stop its caresses.

"Very poor repayment for such loyalty, I think," Aunt Penny replied.

"Why me?" I asked.

"Brett trained her to be yours. He did a very good job of it too."

"I don't understand."

"In some way he acquired one of your old boots and gave it to her when she was being weaned. She learned your scent and this is her comfort now, to be near you."

"He'll have to un-learn her then." I sighed as the dog nuzzled my hand.

I looked at Aunt Penny. "Will you please tell me just what happened? Bessie—"

"That sweet little feather-wit!" exclaimed Aunt Penny. "She's less help than nothing. I do feel sorry for Malcolm sometimes, that dear boy."

"Please, Aunt Penny?" I asked again.

"You were out on the terrace with the duke. Do you remember that?"

I nodded in agreement.

"When you turned to come in to the drawing room, you tripped and fell over his great dog. You hit your head on that marble pedestal right beside the doorway and landed on your arm in such a way as to have broken it in two places. Brett was absolutely in a panic. He insisted on carrying you up here himself and then he took off right away for London to get a doctor. Tyler told him that we could send for Doctor Smythe but Kilnarne insisted you must have the best available. I don't think the doctor was best pleased at being rousted out to come here to the country just to fix a broken arm but Brett wouldn't hear otherwise. Said your arm must not be disfigured because of him. We were more worried about your poor head because we couldn't awaken you for such a long time."

I lay still, digesting this information. At last I asked, "Is Brett still here?"

"Yes, he's with the boys. Refused to leave until he could talk to you and make his apologies. Shall I send him up to you?"

"No," I whispered and again the tears began.

Aunt Penny misinterpreted the cause and asked anxiously, "Does it hurt again?"

"No. Please make him go away. Please?"

"My dear, it's rather difficult to make a duke do anything he doesn't want to. And there isn't anyone here big enough to throw him out, even if they would. He's been no trouble to us and unfailingly kind and helpful. And so worried about you. It's plain to see that he is besotted with you."

"I think I'm hungry. Might I have a bowl of soup? I dreamed of one once."

Aunt Penny looked bewildered. "Dreamed of soup? How strange. Let me go and see. Cook has been making custard and planning omelets and steamed fish and other delights in anticipation of you wanting to eat. Shall I call someone to stay with you?"

"No I'm not afraid to stay by myself. Take Beloved with you. What a silly name for a dog."

"My dear she won't leave unless she wants to. Silly or not, you are her beloved, just as she is yours."

"Did the doctor approve of a dog in the sickroom?" I asked.

Aunt Penny chuckled a bit. "He was a little startled by her but said he could see no reason why not. She has been perfectly content to stay on the foot of the bed and not disturb you. Perhaps if you were ill rather then injured… But as it is, he said she could stay."

"I'm still hungry Aunt Penny," I reminded her.

As she left the room, I thought to push Beloved out of the way but found my hand caressing her instead.

Aunt Penny was quiet as she entered the room, as if she expected me to be sleeping again. But I was much too hungry to sleep. The tray held several bowls, some warm and wonderful-smelling bread rolls and a vase with one perfect yellow rose.

I discovered to my dismay that I could not sit up because of the boards tied to my arm, so Aunt Penny fed me with a spoon. Never again shall I taste anything as delicious as that bowl of chicken broth and the fresh bread that went with it. In between bites of bread was more lemonade. It seemed a veritable feast!

Aunt Penny smiled at me. "I have another bowl of soup if you wish, or there is the custard."

"More soup please," I said as I opened my mouth in anticipation.

Instead, she brought the rose over to my nose and waited for me to sniff it.

"What are you doing?" I inquired.

"It's from Brett. With his love, he asked me to tell you."

I closed my eyes. "Am I to eat that as well?"

"No, dear." She chuckled and continued, "I thought you might like to have a closer look at it. It's such a pretty thing."

"I'd rather have more soup, if you don't mind."

More soup, more bread, more lemonade and then the custard. Absolute bliss! I sighed and snuggled down into the bed. Beloved snuggled even closer to me. I peered down at her.

"When does she eat?" I asked.

"Everyone takes turns at bringing her food when they come up to see you." Aunt Penny smiled at me, then at the dog.

"Do you mean to say that this has been an exhibition hall?" My voice wavered as I asked her this. "And with me in my nightclothes?"

"Oh no dear. Just the family and Malcolm and Brett of course."

"Of course," I groaned.

"Bertie, my dear, you must not take him in such dislike. He has done nothing—"

"Nothing but make my life one great misery ever since he first appeared here. I shall take him in whatever dislike I wish. And his dogs!"

"But—"

"No enough. I wish to sleep." I turned my head away from her and closed my eyes. The tears came anyway and I heard myself sob. Beloved whined in reply.

The next day however, I felt almost a new woman and wished to try to sit up. The protests at such a foolish idea soon convinced me to save my breath. The doctor would say when I might sit up or move or do anything.

I must not rush but only wait for his return. My waking periods became longer as I slept less. Meals were still soup and custard and every tray contained one yellow rose in a vase.

That evening Nick came to visit. He took my good hand and kissed it then leaned down and kissed my cheek. "Well my girl, you gave us a real fright! Feeling more the thing are you?"

"Yes but I do wish I could at least sit up. It's the outside of enough having to just lie here flat all the time."

"The doctor promised to call tomorrow. If you pass his inspection, who can say what you may be allowed to do?" He looked at my arm, encased in its boards. "Does your arm hurt, Bertie?"

"No I don't think so. I can't even move it or lift it, it's just a great lump."

"How about your poor head?" he asked.

"I don't think I would be too happy in bright sunlight and if I try to turn it too quickly I wish I had not. But it's much better."

"Aunt Penny says you remembered what happened?"

"Yes. I wish I—" I came to a halt as a question occurred to me. "Nick why are you here?"

"Why shouldn't I be here when you were hurt so badly? Fine brother I should be to not come to you."

"That's not what I mean. How did you know?"

"Brett told me when he came to town for the doctor. Splendid chap."

"Which one?" I asked.

"Both of course." He laughed at the look of confusion on my face.

"Nick, er, did you really… Brett said, um…" I could feel the flush mounting in my face.

"Did I or we what?" His laugh had awakened Beloved and her tail was thumping me again.

"Did you give him permission to court me?" I whispered.

"Well of course. Why not? He's everything I was hoping to find for you. Although I never thought to look as high as a duke, I will admit. But you're worthy of him."

"No I'm not."

"Bertie." The tone of his voice was severe. "I know you've just had a tremendous knock on your head but I wish you wouldn't talk such foolishness." Beloved was inching her way to my hand and I moved it in irritation.

"Why couldn't you have at least asked me for my opinion?"

"What? I would have wagered that you were in love with him five years ago."

"That was five years ago. I told you in London before I came back home, that I had no wish to marry."

"Oh well young girls frequently say that kind of thing. But they don't really mean it."

"Nick I did mean it. I did and I do. Look what you've done—"

"Bertie, what are you rambling on about? You're not wed yet, are you?"

"I don't know," I wailed.

"You don't know? What are you saying?"

"That great lummox does not listen to anything I say. He just stands there and smiles at me and says I will love him and I will love Castle Kilnarne and how do I know what he may have done since you have evidently given him the freedom of my bedchamber?"

"What?" Nick shouted and jumped from his chair so rapidly that it went over backward. Beloved sat up and barked at him, which startled both of us. Nick picked up the chair but as he started to sit in it again, Beloved jumped over me and, leaning precariously over the edge of the bed as a barrier between us, howled ferociously at him.

The door to my room crashed open and in rushed Tyler, Malcolm and, as I should have known, His Grace.

They stood there looking from one to the other of us, Beloved still barking but in a more sedate, dignified way. Brett raised his hand and in a very soft voice said, "Quiet." She closed her mouth and lay down beside me, looking up at him.

Tyler was the first to speak. "Are you all right, Bertie?"

I started to laugh. I felt like a Bedlamite but I couldn't help myself. Nick looked at his feet, then frowned at me. He looked at each our visitors in turn.

"Er, ah, Bertie said something that startled me and I tipped my chair over. Then that da—dog began to bark at me. I-I'd never heard her bark before. Surprised me, that's all. Nothing else happened."

I was suddenly tired from all the excitement. I looked at Nick and asked, "Will you please send me one of the aunts? I feel the greatest desire to sleep. Good night, gentlemen." I closed my eyes to avoid looking at any of them. I wiggled my fingers slightly and Beloved came over to me, nestling under my hand. I didn't even hear the men leave the room.

Chapter Eleven

&

An unfamiliar voice awakened me. I opened my eyes and turned my head to look at the visitor. Only after having done so, did I realize that there was no longer any discomfort in doing so. I frowned at the gray-haired man leaning over me and whispered, "Who are you?"

"Well lassie, you're much more the thing than the last time I saw you." He took my hand and leaned down to peer intently into my eyes. I shrank back against the pillows. "Ah-h-h," he said to whatever he saw there. He reached over to touch my head and I winced. "Not yet, eh?" he asked.

"Who—?" I mumbled.

He released my hand and sat down in the nearby chair. "I'm Doctor Martin. Brought here by His Grace to tend to your hurts." He shook his head in remembrance. "Never met so determined a man. But you had a good knock on the head, lassie and that arm—" His voice faded away. "Well now then," he said briskly. "Let's just have a look at that head." He turned and signaled for Aunt Cassie to come forward. "If you'll just help me remove this bandage then," and he turned around to lift a big black bag onto the chair.

Aunt Cassie bent and kissed my cheek. "Lie still, dear. I'll be as gentle as I can."

I had not realized that there was a bandage on my head and was amazed as she unwrapped and unwound it. Tears nestled in her eyes but they didn't spill over. I closed my eyes as I waited for whatever was to come.

Gentle hands fluttered over the tender area above my forehead and just to the left of my left eye. I opened my eyes and was surprised to discover that the hands were those of the doctor. "Nasty, that," was all that he said. He picked up a bottle from the table and with surprising gentleness daubed some of the contents on my head and into my hair. "Miracle it wasn't worse," he said to no one in particular. "Now we'll just wrap that up again and then have a look at that arm." He hummed a tuneless little song under his breath as he bustled about. I felt strange movements about my head and closed my eyes again.

I moved my feet lazily and felt no obstruction. "Beloved?" I asked the room.

"She's out for her walk, dear," Aunt Cassie said. "Otherwise the doctor could not be touching you."

"Oh," I said.

With a last gentle pat the doctor finished whatever he was doing to my head. Going around to the other side of the bed he reached for the boarded-up arm. He looked around and asked Aunt Cassie, "Is there another pillow that we can put under this arm?"

"I'll just go get one," she said and left the room.

"What happened to my arm?" I asked. "Why is it encased in boards like this?"

"I didn't see how you fell, you know. But you landed on it in such a way as to have broken both bones in the lower arm, plus the upper arm just above the elbow. Never saw such a thing, except in war, of course. Suspect you may have landed on something hard with it bent and it just snapped." He was carefully inspecting his work to make sure that nothing had moved or dislodged itself. "The boards are something new. Keep it still until completely healed and the arm should be straight and not shorter than the other." His voice became more stern as he added, "You must not try to move it yourself, now."

Aunt Cassie came back just then with an armful of pillows. The doctor carefully examined them and finally selected one. He punched it and said with satisfaction, "This one should do just fine." He looked at Aunt Cassie and said, "Now then, when I lift the arm you put the pillow under it, just so." With extreme gentleness he placed both hands under my arm and carefully lifted it as Aunt Cassie deftly placed the pillow under it.

"Does that hurt you at all lass?" he asked.

"No it just looks so funny," I replied. "Sticking up in the air like that. But if I could just sit up sometimes?" I asked wistfully.

He looked at me intently. "Well just for a while perhaps." I started to move myself and he said, "No wait. Let me think for a moment." He studied the entire length of me with a frown on his face, then suddenly smiled. "Just a moment," he said.

He walked over to the door, opened it and shouted, "My lords? Your Grace? Your help, if you'd be so kind?"

I looked up in wonder as Nick, Tyler, Malcolm and Kilnarne entered the room.

The doctor scrutinized and then addressed them all. "I think that Lady Bertie may sit up just a bit but she must not attempt such a thing by herself. She's liable to do damage to that arm. If she is carefully lifted while someone else lifts her arm and there is a pillow at hand to put under it so there is no strain, no strain on the arm at all, I think it may be done." He came over to the side of the bed. "Now then, Lord Hadleigh, you lift the arm and Your Grace, you come here and gently lift her under the arms. Gently, I say and only just a little."

The men obediently took their places. I closed my eyes in mortification wishing I had not started all this fuss. I opened them again as Nick gently grasped my arm, not lifting it yet as he looked at Brett. With more gentleness than I had thought him capable of possessing, Brett's huge hands gripped me carefully, but with the least amount of pressure and I suddenly found myself to be sitting up. Malcolm quickly placed the pillow under my arm as Aunt Cassie inserted another one behind my back.

The men backed away with pleased looks on their faces and Brett regarded me with a singularly sweet smile. "Lady Bertie," he said, "you can have no idea how delighted I am to see you doing so much better!"

I was quite out of breath and leaned my head back on the pillows. "Thank you all," I whispered.

The doctor said, "Now then, you see how it is to be done? And for down, just reverse the procedure. If the arm is to regain its normal strength and straightness it must be kept absolutely still. She must not attempt to move herself for at least a month."

I groaned at this pronouncement and at the thought of Brett staying here all that time. Would I never be rid of him?

"Are you all right, Bertie?" asked Nick.

"She's just a little dizzy, probably," answered the doctor. "First time her head's been up in a week, you know." A week! There was obviously much I didn't know about this entire matter.

A shuffling noise at the door proved to be Beloved returning from her walk escorted by a footman. Brett snapped his fingers at her and she ran to him, her tail wagging. He leaned down and patted her head and carefully lifted her to the foot of the bed. She sank down and looked up at me. I would be willing to swear that she smiled at me, on seeing me in my new position. Her tail thumped lightly against my feet. I wiggled my fingers and she crawled up to place her head under my hand and whuffled happily as she settled down.

The men all had silly smiles on their faces as they watched this activity, standing motionless around the bed. The doctor was the first to speak. "I'll be back again in two days to see what further progress you've made." He turned and shook a finger at me. "You may sit up as you are for one hour or so, not more than that, three times a day mind. If you get too tired, get some help and lie down again." He leaned over to pick up my hand and Beloved growled at him, sort of under her breath, if you will.

"Here now we'll have none of that, missy," he said, as he looked sternly at her. "That wasn't part of our bargain." She subsided but never looked away from him until he returned my hand back to the bed. She licked it and looked back at me.

"Bertie dear, are you hungry?" Aunt Cassie asked.

"Oh yes, I am," I responded.

"Come then, all you men, out of the way. Let the girl rest, while I get her something to eat." And she shooed them all out of the room, leaving Beloved and me to commune with each other.

* * * * *

The next two days passed quickly in a whirl of up in the bed and then down again, visitors for short periods and one or the other of the aunts bringing me trays of food. I knew that I was getting better because I was so ravenous. There were two major aggravations, the continuing presence of Brett and the yellow rose that still appeared with regularity on the tray carrying my meals. Without my asking, Aunt Penny was careful to always accompany Brett when he came for his very short visits.

I had never before been so constrained, nor suffered such a long period of inactivity. The boredom finally caused me to welcome even Brett to my room, although I was even happier when he left. He was punctiliously polite and unfailingly cheerful as he entertained me with some small story he deemed amusing. He kissed my hand when he entered and again when he took his leave but made no attempt at further physical contact to my great relief. His great green eyes twinkled as they inspected me, threatening to engulf me in their depths. I suspected that if he didn't soon leave Hadleighwoode, I should find myself mesmerized against my will. He made a point of staying with me for not longer than five or ten minutes and I heaved a great sigh of relief at his exit.

The next visit by the doctor was a quick one. He assured us that in a month or so I should be able to sit in a chair and in another month or so after that I might go downstairs. I was elated at the news.

He carefully stripped the great bandage from my head and smiled with pleasure at what he observed. "I think perhaps we might leave this off now," he said as he handed the bandage to Aunt Penny.

With a fumbling hand, I reached up and across to touch my head. He spied me out of the corner of his eye and gently struck my hand away. "Here now," he said. "We'll have none of that, if you please." He scowled at me. "I'd like to leave that open but if you're bound to touch it, I'll have to cover it again. Which is it to be lassie?"

"Sorry," I mumbled. "I just—"

"Plenty of time for that. Don't worry about it just yet. Next week, maybe. Just you eat and regain your strength for now."

"Yes doctor," I said. "Thank you."

He was halfway to the door when he turned and spoke to me. "No matter how good you feel, you will not try to get out of that bed before I return. Is that clear? I shall tell the others the same thing, so don't think to pull the wool over their eyes, either." Without waiting for my reply he left the room.

"Aunt Penny?" I called.

"Yes dear, I'm right here," she replied.

"Aunt Penny, could I have a mirror to see my head?"

A strange look flittered across her face. "I, er, well, dear, I don't think you should, um—" Her voice faded away.

"Is it that bad, then?"

"As the doctor said dear, you took a nasty knock. I cannot believe that it would do you much good to see it just yet. In another week or so, when the discoloration has—"

"Discoloration?" I whispered.

"Of course. Did you think you could knock your head on a marble pedestal and not sustain a bruise from it?"

"I guess I never thought much about it."

"Well don't fret yourself, now. It's much less than it was already." She bustled around the room doing little nonsense things.

I shuddered at the thought of my appearance and what my visitors must have thought about it.

As if she was reading my mind, Aunt Penny said, "We were all so happy that you would be all right your looks were of least concern to us, I do assure you." And with that I had to be content.

There was a small noise at the door and Nick stuck his head around it, frowning at my undressed head. "How are you feeling, now, Bertie? Up to a little talk, perhaps?" He walked over to the chair and as he sat down, Aunt Penny gave my pillow one last plump and went to the door.

"My dear," she said, "I shall not be far away if you should want anything." She smiled at us and left the room.

"Hello Nick. Do I really look such a fright? The doctor says I must not touch my head and I am imagining such horrible things."

"No, no. We are all so pleased, truly, that you will not be marked in any way." He looked around the room. "Where is your companion?" he asked.

"I think she's out for her walk. It's easier for the doctor if she's not here whenever he is."

"Bertie, we need to talk. Do you feel up to it? It can wait— but I rather think that in this case the sooner the better." He was unusually serious.

"What is the matter?" I asked.

"It's Kilnarne."

I felt a surge of hopeful anticipation as I asked, "Is he leaving, then?"

"I don't know, Bertie. That is what we must talk about."

"There is nothing to discuss. I do not love him, I do not wish to marry him and I shall be happy to see the last of him."

"I don't understand you, my girl. Why have you taken him in such dislike? He's—"

I interrupted him. "He's overbearing, he doesn't listen to me, he's a great, huge, bufflehead!" Nick's mouth fell open at this statement but I raised my good hand to keep him silent. "I was perfectly serious when I told you I had no wish to marry and for the life of me I can not fathom why you gave him permission to court me. Not that he has, exactly," I added as an afterthought. "I only wish he would go away."

"Just what do you propose to do with yourself if you don't marry?" Nick asked. "I thought all women wished to marry."

"This one doesn't," I stated with emphasis.

"But why not?"

"I just don't."

"But you did?"

"When I was young and foolish, perhaps."

Nick's laughter interrupted me. "Yes," he chortled, "you are so old, now. Let me see, you are all of one and twenty, are you not?"

"You know very well I am," I muttered.

"What can have changed your mind, then? I could have sworn that when you came to London you were not averse to the idea." His eyes opened wide at a sudden thought. "Never say you let foolish gossip change your mind?"

"No. It was not that."

"But it was something that happened in London?"

"No. I was unhappy there, I admit. But it was nothing specific, truly, Nick. I just came to realize when I came back home that I would be happier here than anywhere else. Can't I please just stay here?" I pleaded.

"Do you mean here at Hadleighwoode or the Dower House? Of course, you may have the Dower House as long as you wish. But you must remember, Hadleighwoode really must be considered as Joan's and mine. My country seat, if you will."

"But Joan hates it here," I protested.

"Be that as it may, it is nevertheless my country seat. And in this case Joan's wishes must come before yours, as you do have the Dower House where you may do as you please."

"Oh." I thought about his words. "Does Joan wish me not to be here, then?" I asked. "Does she wish me to leave?" I could not hide the quiver in my voice.

"Of course she doesn't," he consoled me. "But neither does she wish to see you on the shelf and remaining a spinster, you know."

We sat in silence for several moments. Nick cleared his throat. "What am I to tell Kilnarne? I did give him my permission, you know."

"But you never even asked me!" I wailed.

"It isn't in the normal course of events for me to have to ask you. I was sure that you would find in him everything you could want—"

"But I didn't!"

"Then tell me what you do want," he replied in a reasonable manner. "I must tell him something." He looked at me and continued. "He has really been most distraught about your accident, Bertie. He insisted on going to London to get the best doctor—"

"And set a record for time, I know, I know," I muttered. "I've heard all about that, several times." My irony was lost on him. "Just tell him to go back to Ireland. Anywhere."

"Bertie!" His voice suddenly had an edge to it.

"Please, Nick, just tell him I—" My voice died away.

"Tell him what?"

"I, er." I turned my head away from him.

Concern tempered his voice as he asked, "Are you all right?"

"I am as all right as I may be, under the circumstances. I just wish him to go away. Is that so much to ask?"

"Bertie, the man is so in love with you that if you asked him to go to, ah, to the Antipodes I'm sure he would." Now his hand came up to silence me. "But I am sure he would not go anywhere without a reason. And so far, you have not come up with one. Bertie, no man worthy of the name would just go away without a reason. I will cry off for you but I must know why. Is that really so much to ask of you?"

In a very small voice, I asked, "Could he not go away while I think?"

Nick's laugh rang through the room. "Oh Bertie, what am I to do with you? Was I so wrong in thinking that all those years ago—?"

I interrupted him. "Please, Nick?"

He stood up and looked down at me. "Bertie, it is an honor for him to pay his addresses to you and for him to be a guest in our home. I cannot and will not insult the man by your foolishness."

"But that's it!" I cried.

"What's it? What are you talking about?"

The words tumbled out of my mouth and Nick touched a finger to my lips. "Slow down. I cannot understand a word of your babble. Now take a deep breath and begin again, please."

"I, er, you know that we are well-born, I admit that, but I am not well enough born to become a duchess. Such fustian! His head—"

Again the chair fell as he vaulted from it, a look of fury on his face. In a clipped voice, he said, "I think your head is still affected by your accident. You...we...are well enough born to match with anyone, even royalty, if we and they wished. Such nonsense I have never heard and never thought to hear from one of my own family. I would not insult His Grace by even mentioning such a thing and I hope you may not either!"

"But I already did!" The words escaped my mouth before I had realized it and, in futility, covered my mouth with my good hand. "Oh," I said, as I cowered back against the pillow.

"No I will not strike you, although I am tempted. But if ever again you say such a nonsensical thing to anyone— anyone!" he bellowed, "I will not be responsible for what I may do." He reached down and straightened the chair and without another word, stalked from the room.

I closed my eyes but the tears streamed down my face anyway and I fell asleep.

Chapter Twelve

ᔕᑎ

During the next two weeks I proceeded to turn myself into the most miserable person in the entire realm. My mind whirled in every direction as I belabored and cudgeled it to find an excuse that would be acceptable to Nick and deter the advances of Brett. Perhaps if I had been allowed out of my bed I would not have become so irritable. Frustration combined with impatience at my inability to come up with such an excuse turned me into a termagant and within two days the only person in the entire household who would or could put up with me for more than two minutes at a stretch was His Grace.

Three days after my confrontation with Nick I was so lonely that I was almost glad to see Brett. Whether Nick thought that proximity would change my mind, or was assured that Brett was a gentleman above all things, I never knew but for whatever reason, Brett was allowed to sit in my room for as long a time as he or I wished. The aunts were so disgusted with my behavior that they stayed away from me except for their nursing duties. By my foolishness I compromised myself several times over by being so much alone with Brett in my room.

I was short-tempered. I screamed. I cried. I threw anything I could reach that was small enough to throw, or I sat in morose silence, refusing to answer any questions asked of me. I did, however, continue to eat any food that was presented. And through it all amazingly he sat there with that interminable smile on his big face, his green eyes glinting with humor and told me stories in such a hypnotic voice that I could feel myself day by day falling right into his carefully prepared trap. I hated him and I hated myself.

Beloved did indeed become my beloved. She never reproached me and was always content with a smile or a touch. I lay there and watched her grow. She was a beautiful animal. We forged a bond in that room that remained unbroken for nearly twenty years. What an insidious trick Brett played on us when he gave her to me!

Kilnarne would kiss my hand when he arrived and again when he left but did not touch me otherwise. The easy smile never left his face and I began to wonder if he were lack-witted indeed. He was everything that was patient and kind, however, no matter how shrewish I became.

That third day when he came to sit by me, he handed me a small box on which was one yellow rose. I didn't want either and told him so in very plain words but my wishes were for nothing. When he persisted in my opening and keeping the contents, I finally conceded defeat and drew in my breath when I saw the tiny jade horse.

"Oh no, Your Grace, this is much too valuable. I could not keep it," I protested.

His laugh filled the room. "No, it's worthless!" he exclaimed.

That made me more angry. How dare he give me something he considered worthless? "How so?" I asked, coldly.

"Turn it over. Crack along the bottom. No good for anything." he said in all seriousness and like a looby I believed him, so I accepted it. Years later I discovered it was a natural flaw in the jade which enhanced the value rather than detracted from it.

He kept me so off balance during those next two weeks, I began to wonder if I were the lack-wit. The day after the jade horse, it was a bolt of the most glorious golden-hued silk for a ball gown and the blond lace to complement it. I knew this to be extremely valuable but he assured me he'd been given it by one of the "gentlemen" for a favor received. Since smuggling was still a gainful occupation in many parts of England, I believed him and started planning in my mind how the gown should be made up. Of course, I later found out that he'd never even seen a smuggler!

The next day it was a carving he had made out of a piece of driftwood. Clearly worthless, so we avoided any argument for that day. A copy of the latest piece of music for the pianoforte by Mr. Beethoven was followed by a lovely, carved ivory fan, which was followed by a Norwich shawl, which was followed by the largest set of watercolors I had ever seen.

Next was a little leather-bound volume of poems by Byron, then a collar and lead for Beloved and a huge shell from the sea, which, when held to my ear, had the sound of the waves in it. A singing bird in a cage was solemnly presented on the next day and that was followed by a piece of quartz rock that sparkled in the sun. The last gift totally perplexed me when I opened it and a batch of multicolored embroidery silks fell out and spilled all over the bed. The piece of linen accompanying it had dark lines scrawled all over it and I held it every way to decipher the picture.

"What in the world is it?" I asked.

"My family crest. What else would it be?" And he carefully identified all the individual emblems and told me what colors each should be worked in.

"But why give this to me?"

"Every duchess makes one," was his smug reply.

A large groan was my only answer.

Each of these presents was accompanied by one perfect yellow rose and I began to think that all yellow roses should be banned from the world. He always wore gold or brown or yellow, except when he was in formal evening dress, his dogs were gold, his hair was gold. I was heartily sick of it all. I remembered the gold silk and loathed it and him and everything else in the world that was gold. Although I tried very hard not to, I also couldn't help but recall Madame Zorina and her prophecies.

After the ceremony of the present each day he would sit at his ease and talk and talk and talk. I learned more than I had ever wanted to know about Ireland, the Yorkist kings and the Lancastrian kings and Castle Kilnarne and Irish wolfhounds and society—from his view at least—and things I had never even heard of.

If I didn't want to hear about horses then he talked about dogs. If I didn't want to know about hunting then he talked about dancing. If I didn't want to hear about real people then he talked about the "little people" of Ireland.

Brett's size and his coloring naturally prompted me to ask if there was Plantagenet blood in his heritage. He seemed to me a veritable reincarnation of Edward IV, or Henry VIII. To my surprise, his face flushed a little and for the only occasion in the time I had known him, he was at a loss for words. I was confused. Surely after all these years, such a possibility should not be embarrassing. There were many people who contrived that their family tree should show them as a bastard branch of some royal house or another.

"It is a possibility, Lady Bertie. Richard's father was Lord Lieutenant of Ireland before Richard was born and Plantagenets were not usually well known for their constancy." He hung his head for a moment then raised his green eyes back up to me. "Would it matter to you if it were true?" he asked in a, for him, very quiet voice.

Now I was confused. "No. Why should it? It just seemed a likely chance. I do remember enough history to know that Richard of York was in Ireland and since you are also from Ireland and with your coloring and your size—" My voice broke off.

Fortunately at that moment we were interrupted by Bessie and Mal, who came rushing in to tell us about the recovery of Silverton's Pride. Mal had that morning put him through his paces for the first time since Pride had come up lame. They were all exuberance at his regained speed. It was now certain that Pride would be entered in the Derby and they could talk of little else.

I should have liked to go see the horse but then I should have liked to go anywhere. Bessie begged Brett to accompany them to the stable to see for himself. After a strange look at me, Brett agreed to go with them and I was suddenly furious at being left all alone.

When he came to see me the next day I was cold to him at first but he soon jollied me out of my mood, telling me of Bessie and Mal and the Pride. His laugh challenged me to remain sullen but I lost that battle too.

He educated me about Greek and Roman mythology — and promised to take me someday to see the original sites of these stories — theatre in London and Paris, with a side lecture on the plays of Mr. Shakespeare. His favorite was *The Taming of the Shrew*, but as he explained it, I quite failed to see the humor in it. He was familiar with the current musical scene and described the famous opera houses of the world. The Royal Academy and its exhibiting artists, not to mention the great sculptures of Italy and Greece, German castles, French ballet, the Scottish Highlands — nothing missed his consideration. And I missed none of it either.

Brett was as fluent in French as I was and we spent one complete afternoon conversing entirely in that lilting language. There seemed to be nothing he had not seen, no place of importance that he had not visited and I was more and more bewildered by his pursuit of me. Although he did not actively press his suit, I was not allowed to forget it, either.

I succeeded in raising his ire, only slightly, one day. When, my mind reeling by his recitation of places visited and things seen, I asked in confusion, "How old are you anyway? It seems impossible for one person to have done so much in so few years."

The glint of humor that was always in his eyes left them for only a moment, then returned. "I am four and thirty. It is possible to see much of the world in thirteen years if one keeps one's eyes open. Do you think the Irish to still be savages, then?"

"No, of course not!" I replied. "It is just that, er, you seem to have spent so much time in traveling but yet your estate is apparently a large one and must surely require some of your time..." My voice dwindled away.

"It is a matter of knowing in whom to place your trust and making it worthwhile for them to continue trusting in me. Nick does the same, does he not? His estate is as large as mine, or nearly so."

I learned that he had two younger brothers and one younger sister. His mother was still the chatelaine of Castle Kilnarne. I would certainly love them all, as they would love me.

And through all those wonderful, horrid days, I could not come up with any acceptable excuse to keep from becoming his wife. I fretted and became ever more miserable. If it had been my leg that was encased in boards instead of my arm, I am positive that I should have joyfully used both hands and strangled him at least ten times each day.

Nothing I could do or say changed his mind. I insulted him on more than one occasion and it had absolutely no effect on him. He would merely respond, "I know how you must feel being so cooped up, so I will just disregard your words.

We were saved from total warfare only by the reappearance of the doctor. He was pleased by my spirit and my obvious good health other than my arm. It was his opinion that I might be allowed now to get out of bed and sit in a chair. I was ecstatic!

I nearly swooned when I tried it, however and again Brett came to the rescue. He would have carried me there but the doctor was afraid I might strain my arm, so Brett had to be content with shepherding me to the chair. He was so big that it seemed not at all difficult for him to be on both sides of me at once, carefully supporting my good arm with one big hand and my boarded arm with his other one.

Beloved jumped and danced as she accompanied us to the chair and made happy little whimpering noises in her throat. She was by now as tall as my knees and I shuddered to realize how big she would be when she was grown.

My disposition improved mightily once I was allowed out of my bed and I began to take an interest in my appearance. The only time I had been allowed a mirror, Aunt Penny had craftily waited until it was near dark and had then placed the candle in the wrong area for me to see clearly. I was so entranced with my blackened eyes and forehead that I had not noticed the area of my head that had been damaged.

Now however, I could place myself where I could see clearly what had been done to me and dropped the mirror in shock when I'd had a good look. Fortunately it fell on Beloved who was sitting at my feet. I say fortunately only because it didn't break. She was not very happy with me for a time but I finally managed to convince her that I had not done it on purpose and was truly sorry.

My head had hit the marble pedestal just into the area covered by my hair and above the temple. The skin was broken, so my head had been shaved in a rather large area. This was now covered by a short fuzz. The doctor assured me that it would soon grow out and the scar would be hidden by my hair. It was small comfort until he pointed out how much worse it would have been had I cracked my skull.

I cringed as I thought about those first days of convalescence when I had been the prime exhibit and marveled at the composure of my family at what must have been a horrendous sight. And Brett! I should never again be able to face him without thinking of this. And then I remembered that I didn't want to face him again. But I felt my chances of accomplishing such a feat to be very slim, indeed.

* * * * *

The wedding of Bessie and Mal had been set for the first week in September and plans had been proceeding despite my possible inability to participate. Bessie was adamant that I should stand with her while poor Malcolm, to avoid having to choose between Nick, Tyler or Brett, chose Harry instead.

Bessie's bride gown had been finished and was now hanging in her wardrobe. She would go and look at it and caress its silken folds, as if to reassure herself that it was not all a dream. When she saw the golden silk that Brett had given me, she immediately decided that I must have that made up for my gown. I could not imagine how I should wear any kind of gown with my arm still in its boards but my concerns were of no importance to her or to anyone else, either.

I had never been particularly vain but I could not accept that I should appear in public with my head as it was. The fuzz grew longer and began to cover the scar. And, of all things, the fuzz turned into curls! It would still be very short but perhaps I might with the help of the hairdresser contrive something. My hair had never been really cut until the accident and I began to consider cutting it all short, like Bessie's, until Brett heard of it. His proclamation forbidding such an action was daunting, to say the least. The decision was finally made that I might cut the hair on the other side of my head to match that already cut but only that portion in front of my ears. The rest must remain as it was.

With great trepidation—and my eyes closed—I allowed the hairdresser and his scissors to begin. The great, long and heavy locks fell and were quickly snatched up by Brett, who was, of course, an observer. Bessie was on my other side patting my hand in comfort and offering words of advice to the hairdresser, who only grunted at her in reply.

My head felt suddenly lighter and I was not sure why. It might have been the excitement of the activity, or simply the decreased weight of my hair. I scrunched my eyes tighter. The steady hands of the hairdresser gently fluttered around my head. I felt a drop of water on my cheek and for once it was not from tears. I heard a murmured sigh and Bessie squealed in delight.

"Only look, Bertie!" she said as she placed a mirror in my hand. "It's truly going to curl, just like the other side."

Cautiously I opened my eyes and looked in the mirror and was astounded at what I saw. All around my face were feathers of curls, which at one and the same time softened my face and made my eyes much larger than I had ever noticed them to be. I preened openly for the first time in my life, looking first one way into the mirror, then the other. My eyes were drawn to Brett's and seeing in them a smile of approval, I laughed wildly.

He said only, "Don't think to do more than that, will you?"

Bessie ran to him and ruffled his curls, then her own, laughing as she did so. "Don't you think Bertie should have curls like we do, Your Grace?" Her flirtatious way with him startled me but he only laughed at her and a niggling little thought deep within me made me look at both of them with a different eye. But his eyes were on me throughout and I decided not to worry about it.

Brett closeted himself with the doctor when next that gentleman appeared, with the immediate result of my being allowed to walk a bit, provided that someone — usually Brett — carried my arm for me. I tried to practice by myself in my room but found that the weight of the boards soon pulled so at my shoulder that I could not continue. I could not balance well enough to support the arm by myself, so I was pleased — in a disgusted way — at the continued attentions of His Grace.

He also closeted himself with the dressmaker who was called to Hadleighwoode to start my silk gown. He would not tell me what he was about, however, no matter how many times I asked.

One lovely sunny evening, about two weeks before the wedding, Brett asked me if I'd like to go out to the terrace for a while. My head swam with dizziness at the very thought of it. The aunts were set to find some way in which to dress me for my excursion. They solved the problem very easily by simply removing the sleeve entirely from an old dress and then pinning the dress around me.

Brett and Bessie came to get me. I wondered how we should manage it when Brett turned to Bessie and said, "When Bertie stands, I shall pick her up and you must carefully place her arm on top of her." Then, to me, "I shall be as easy as I may, Bertie but if you feel any discomfort, please tell me." He took a deep breath and said to both of us, "Now!"

I found myself engulfed in his great arms and Bessie, on tiptoe, gently placed my arm across my body. I felt as though I were a piece of thistledown. Bessie ran ahead and prepared the way for us. Beloved brought up the rear as we trailed down the hall, down the great stairway and out through the drawing room doors.

A great cheer went up as he strode through the doors and he stopped there to acknowledge it. I turned my head slowly from side to side and was astounded at the gathering. All of the servants, the family and even the Squire's family were there to greet me. Blondel stood to one side slowly wagging his tail.

Brett carefully lowered me to a chair and Aunt Penny placed a pillow under my arm, while Tyler placed a footstool beneath my feet. I felt as pampered as a queen! I was speechless, however, as each person greeted me. The emotion overcame me and I found myself laughing and crying at the same time. It was one of the happiest evenings of my life.

Blondel came over and sniffed politely at my arm and his eyes conveyed a silent apology. I scratched his head and he made happy whuffling noises. Beloved would not be left out and placed herself next to the footstool.

It seemed that I had barely become situated when it was time to return to my room. The fresh air and the company were so exhilarating that I could barely keep my eyes open but I resisted until I had not more energy to do so. Once again Brett swept me into his arms and we returned to my chamber.

Instead of lowering me to the bed however, he sat down in the big chair with me on his lap. I looked at him expectantly.

"I am sorry, Miss Bertie," he began and there was a strange emphasis on the word "miss". This was, in itself, very strange as he had up until just recently been most punctilious about calling me "Lady Bertie".

I realized that in the last day or so however, the "Lady" had gone by the wayside leaving just the more intimate "Bertie". I wondered what the next step in his campaign might be. I remained silent as he continued. "I find I must go up to London tomorrow. Some things I alone can do and this is one of them. I will return before the wedding, however and hope to see you even more improved in health."

The formal words sounded strange after his easy banter of the past month and I looked at him questioningly.

"To remind you of me while I am away I have one last little item for you," he said, as he shifted me around on his lap while he looked in various pockets. At last, he pulled a little box from somewhere and handed it to me. To my great relief, this one had no yellow rose on its top.

The top came off easily in my hand and I gasped at the golden beauty of the contents. It was a finely worked chain with a small key dangling from it, as a pendant. The key was worked in a manner similar to filigree out of a yellowish substance that was not metallic. Gently I eased it out of the box and held it up to the light. As I held it in my hand, it became warm to my touch. It made no sense to me whatever.

"What is it?" I whispered.

"The key to my heart," he answered quietly.

I did not know what to do or say, as the key shimmered in the candlelight. Finally I asked, "What is it made of?"

"It is amber, like your eyes." And very gently he leaned down and placed a tender kiss on each of those eyes. I could feel the tears start to well and hoped they would not spill over.

"Why do you do these things, my lord? I have told you—"

"I have been led to believe that women sometimes change their minds. I hope to help you change yours." He nuzzled my cheek.

"Please take it back," I pleaded.

"I had hoped for a present from you before I left, as well." The devilish glint returned to his eyes as he said this and my heart plunged to my feet.

"Your Grace, I—"

"Brett," he whispered softly to the top of my head.

"Brett, I do not wish to—"

He laughed. "Yes, I have heard you say that. I was hoping for something less permanent, shall we say?"

I looked at him in confusion and pulled my head back as his lips lowered to mine and I was captured.

He murmured, "Don't fight me," just before his lips rested on mine. Just as in the garden it was like nothing I had ever experienced and sensations previously unthought-of raced from one end of me to the other. His lips nuzzled, cajoled, enticed, commanded. The butterflies danced on my ears, my chin, the tip of my nose. I discovered that my good arm had wound itself around his neck and was pulling his head even closer to mine. I never wanted to let him go. I was certainly mad. I heard a moan and realized that I was the culprit. I couldn't breathe. I didn't want to. It went on and on and on and—

With one final delicate nibble on my nose, he pulled his head back and looked deep into my eyes. The most glorious smile was on his face as he asked, "Wasn't I right, then?"

I was totally confused by the question. "I don't—" My voice didn't seem to want to work right and the words came out in a husky whisper.

"Told you you'd like to be kissed. I'm usually right about these things, you know. Or do you need another demonstration before you can decide absolutely?" He was still caressing the back of my head, causing shivers all over me.

"Yes, my lord," I breathed. I could recognize defeat when it hit me over the head. In this instance, he was absolutely the winner!

Chapter Thirteen

∞

The excitement of the wedding permeated every inch of the grand old house and I was not excluded. Bessie was still determined to have me stand with her but I did not see how I could do so with my arm still encased in its boards. I could barely walk around my room without feeling the strain on my shoulder. All of my protests fell on deaf ears, however.

Four days before the wedding Brett had still not returned but the family began to return home. Joan and the children, Jon and Mary Anne and Malcolm's brothers filled the house with cheerfulness and laughter. The cook grumbled and the gardeners all complained but no one listened to them, either.

I had not yet been allowed to see my gown and I worried about my arm. How would I manage all of this? Beloved listened to my anguished cries and thumped her tail in reply but could offer no constructive solutions.

At last, on the eve of the great day, Brett returned and the house swirled with excitement. Joan was in such awe of the man that she fairly groveled before him. The children simply adored him and Blondel. I knew he was in the house, yet he did not come to see me and my spirits plummeted.

Finally he was escorted to my chamber by an entourage and I wished I could run to him and throw my arms about him. Carrying a box in his arms, with the ever-present yellow rose on its top, he slowly crossed the room to stand in front of me. As he reached down to me he suddenly remembered the box in his hand and frowned at it. He turned and placed it on a table before returning to me. My heart thumped so loud I was sure he could hear it and I was relieved to see the familiar glint in his eyes. He smiled broadly at me.

"Not up and dancing yet?" he asked.

"But I don't like—" I began and at the memory of something else I had thought I didn't like felt the treacherous reddening of my face.

Brett knew what I was thinking and roared with laughter. He said, "We'll see, love."

The endearment made my pulse race and I wished for nothing so much as to throw everyone else from my room, so I could be held once again in those great arms and have his lips on mine.

He clasped his hands together and looking at the entourage said, "Now then, let's get to work."

My eyes went to the box he had been carrying and he noticed my glance. "No, that's for last. We've other things to do first." A motion of his big hand brought forth the dressmaker carrying the most beautiful gown I had ever seen. I was speechless in admiration. It did have the stylish high waistline but no flowers or ribbons were to be seen anywhere. A rather low, square neckline was trimmed in the creamy lace, as were the billowy, long sleeves that buttoned at the wrist. There was an overskirt slashed open down the front, with three bands of the lace inserted to form a 'V' at the back of a short train. It was simple yet elegant and breathtakingly lovely.

The dressmaker turned the gown around so I could see the back and all the buttons. The overskirt was detachable and fastened to the dress with little decorative buttons all around the waistline. Her eyes glowed with pride as she showed her handiwork. She flushed with pleasure at the applause.

Bessie was bubbling over with joy. "Just look, Bertie! You can be dressed in this very easily because of the way it is made. Isn't it wonderful?"

"But my arm—" I began.

"Never worry about that. Just wait to see what Brett's done about your arm!"

Another of the minions was brought forward with several small boxes. Brett looked at me and said, "I think perhaps this would be easier if you were back on the bed. Your arm still needs to be supported." He pulled me up from the chair and swung me into his arms. I giggled with the joy of it all.

Brett carefully placed me on the bed and I looked up in surprise to see the doctor. "This young scoundrel, ma'am, gave me no peace until I agreed to try his foolish invention here. Don't go getting your hopes up yet, because I have to be convinced it will work before I'll agree to it." He was intently examining my arm as he said this and I wondered what he was going to do.

From his bag he withdrew scissors and cautiously cut the strips of old sheeting which held the boards so tightly to my arm. As he cut the last one, the boards clattered together slightly as they fell away from my arm. Brett immediately clasped my hand, holding my arm still. I looked up at him, then back at my arm again. It felt so strange, all tingly and almost as if it wanted to float across the room now that it was unencumbered.

Tentatively, I wiggled a finger or two and Doctor Martin immediately grasped my hand and said, "No don't try to move it yet." I subsided. Gently he ran his fingers up and down my arm, lingering at the areas that had been broken. He sighed, finally and began to unwind the strips of cloth that had been wound around and around it.

When the last of them fell away he stood there and looked at my arm and seemed pleased with it as well as himself. I turned then to inspect it for myself and was repelled by the whiteness of it. It seemed a pallid and puny thing to me but as he again examined it, a smile lit up his dour face. "Not yet but soon," was all he said.

Brett had the contents of the box in his hands and I frowned at what he held. His smile never wavered as he held out the two pieces of the dress fabric to the doctor. What on earth was this? The doctor held one so that I could get a closer look but it was no help. I still did not know what it was supposed to be.

I felt as though I was at the center stage of the theater, as everyone was once again clustered around the bed. The sense of anticipation was so strong I wished to get on with it. I took the item from the doctor's hand for a closer look and drew in my breath in amazement.

I looked at the doctor. "Do you mean to say that His Grace devised this?" My face reddened as I spoke.

"Yes, he did. You see, the breaks to your arm were above and below the elbow. No reason not to be able to bend your elbow, except that we needed to keep the other bones still. Only way to do that is strap the whole arm. Couldn't have done this if you weren't so close to being healed. Don't know if we can do it now but I said I'd give it a try."

The piece of fabric had been made into a miniature sort of corset, with tucks all around to hold shortened stays in them. There was a little edging of lace at top and bottom and buttonholes up both edges, with a ribbon to draw them together. It would obviously do the work of the bigger boards providing I didn't strain my arm and yet would keep the bones straight while allowing me to wear the beautiful gown and to bend my arm. I should not be able to lift or carry anything but then I shouldn't need to.

It was the most compelling example of love I had ever encountered and I could think of nothing to say that would even begin to be adequate. I looked at Brett, barely able to contain my tears and was dumbfounded to see him blush. I could well imagine the source of his embarrassment. Gentlemen were not supposed to know about corsets and other undergarments worn by ladies, although they might well pay for them. It was easy to see how he might struggle to explain what he wanted made and for why, when he should not even mention the model he had in mind.

In that moment, my fears receded enough that I knew I should be the greatest fool in Christendom if I should lose this man through my stubbornness. I reached up to touch his cheek and murmured, "Yes, Your Grace. Yes." I could tell by the light in his eyes that he knew the question I had just answered and I rejoiced.

The doctor's voice interrupted our reverie. "Well then, don't just stand there gawking. Let's try the blasted things!" Brett carefully lifted my arm and laid the larger piece beneath my upper arm and the smaller one below my forearm. The doctor began to lace them up and threw his hands in the air in disgust. "How you ladies —"

Aunt Penny moved him out of the way. "Here sir, let me try." And she proceeded to thread the ribbons through the buttonholes and draw them up until they were ready to be tied. "How tight should it be?" she asked the doctor.

"Until she winces at it," he muttered. Brett glared at him. I dutifully winced when I felt the pressure but there was no pain.

"There," Aunt Penny said under her breath as she tied the last knot.

"Can you bend your arm?" asked the doctor.

Gingerly, I moved my arm and the freedom of it amazed me. I reached for Brett with it and he gripped my hand with his. I looked at the doctor. "May I get up and walk around?"

"Yes but don't overdo, or you'll still be there tomorrow too. Expect to be dizzy, at first." Brett assisted me from the bed and with his strong arm around me, I paraded around my chamber, showing off my miniature arm corsets to everyone. I was dizzy but I don't think it was just from the standing upright and walking around under my own power. My feet barely touched the floor.

Beloved was whining from all the excitement and I reached to touch her. I felt as though I could conquer anything! I still had my fears but in some way I knew I could overcome them. If I had Brett at my side I could rule the world! The thought of it made me stumble and I was immediately swept up and replaced on the bed. Brett looked at the onlookers and cleared his throat. As if by magic, the room emptied.

For long moments we didn't speak, just looked at each other.

We spoke the same words at the same time, "Dear love," and laughed together.

He took my hand and said only, "When?" My fears came back in full force and I could not look at him.

I knew what he meant and swallowing, said, "I don't know. I'm still afraid and—"

He cleared his throat and said, "You never have to be afraid of me, Bertie."

"I'm not afraid of you, Brett. It's something else entirely. Please don't ask me about it right now. I have to think about it properly. And anyway, we mustn't spoil Bessie's day. She'd be furious with me. And rightly so."

There was again silence for a moment and I ran my hand over my little arm corsets. "However did you come to think of these? They're marvelous!" I looked at him and again surprised the blush.

He stammered, "I...ah...well...the doctor said that your arm must be held straight but you couldn't move it as it was and I cudgeled my poor brain—"

"Poor brain, indeed," I gurgled.

"At any rate the idea just rather came to me and, er—" His voice died away.

I must say I rather enjoyed this discomfited Brett. His overwhelming self-confidence had disguised the gentle side of him. He was obviously not used to being unsure of himself but I reveled in it.

With great difficulty I restrained the laughter that wanted to spill out as I asked him, "And of course, seeing the real-life model gave—"

His chair crashed over as he sprang out of it. Beloved started to bark, then stopped in confusion as she did not know at whom she should be barking, or why. Brett was now blushing furiously.

"Never say such a thing, Bertie!" he pleaded. I whooped with laughter.

"Aha!" I cried, tears rolling down my face. "I see I have found the way to keep you under control. I shall always keep these as a memento just to remind myself."

At last he realized I was truly laughing and straightened the chair and sat back down. "Actually there are two pairs, one for each arm."

"Oh?" I asked sweetly. "Do you intend, then, to break the other arm, my lord?"

The chair went over again as he gasped, "Bertie! How can you say such a thing? I didn't break the first one."

"Maybe not," I mused. "I think it was the pair of you—Blondel and you combined—that were responsible—" My voice died and I gaped in shock as he gripped my shoulders and gently shook me.

The glint was back in his eyes and I laughed up at him. "There then, I have my old Brett back again."

Poor dear, he was so bewildered. He removed his hands as though I had burnt him and stood there looking foolishly at me. His face reddened and he accused, "You said that intentionally."

"Of course, I did." I patted his hand. "You must remember not to be so sure of yourself. Now then, sit down and tell me why two pair of these?"

He made a fuss of adjusting his cravat and his jacket. When he was settled, he said, "Well you see, I could not know whether you might wish to wear them on the outside of your sleeve or under it. They're made to be decorative, so if you wear them outside there is another pair for the other arm. You will not then look off balance."

"Oh Brett," my voice choked. "How thoughtful of you, truly."

"Actually, there is one more piece to your costume."

"Another piece? Where, or should I say, what is it?"

Without a word, he placed what looked to be a shawl on the bed. I picked it up and examined it carefully. It was of the same fabric as the gown, triangular in shape with a lace band inserted across its middle and the lace again around the three edges.

I threw him a quizzical look. "As I said, what is it, a shawl?"

He looked at me and said, "I suppose you could use it for one but I meant it to be a sling. For your arm," he added.

"A sling?" I asked.

"Yes, it ties around your neck to support your arm. You may not need it but if your arm feels tired, then the sling will give it rest and you will not have to hold it so carefully."

It was a lovely present but so were they all. However, by this time I was so exhausted from all the excitement, I found myself yawning. Brett thought this amusing. I no longer cared. I touched the extra arm corsets and said, "Do I wear these while I sleep, now that the other boards are gone?"

"Oh," said Brett. "I don't know. Maybe we should try to put the other boards back."

"Why didn't you have some plain ones made?" I asked. I touched the silk lovingly. "I don't want to ruin these before I wear them."

He rose and went to the door and called to Tyler, who came running. The two men conversed by the door and Tyler left, only to return with the aunts. After some struggles, the original boards were once again in place. I watched Aunt Cassie take the arm corsets and carefully place them on a nearby chest. Aunt Penny shooed the men out of the room over my protests and readied me for sleep.

The anticipation of tomorrow's events made me restless and I feared I should not be able to sleep. But Aunt Penny brought me a posset and almost before I had even quite finished it, I was asleep. I found the empty cup in bed with me in the morning.

* * * * *

Although I slept like the proverbial log I awakened clearheaded and full of tingles. I had asked the aunts to rouse me early as I needed to try on my new gown, in order to decide whether I should wear the arm corsets on the outside of the sleeve or the inside. Because of the way the gown was made, all of this trying on could be done while I was seated in a chair. After much deliberation, I finally chose to wear the upper ones on the outside and the lower ones inside, allowing the full sleeves to bell out.

It was a strangely attractive look and I wondered if I might set a new fashion. Breakfast was brought to me on a tray, as usual and I longed for the time when I might once again join the family. The hairdresser came and did wonders with my hair. The feathery curls around my face were a constant delight to me but I dared not stare at myself in the mirror as much as I wished.

At last I was ready for the gown, now that the arm corsets and my hair were in place. I was allowed to stand this time but when finally I looked in the mirror, I nearly cried. The gown was nearly two inches too long and dragged on the floor all around me. Perhaps if I had not so many tears I might have observed the sly looks of the faces of the aunts but I was too distraught to notice anything except the extra material. It was near time to leave for the little church, so there was not time enough for even the best seamstress in the world to catch up the hem.

There was a knock at the door. "Go away!" I shouted.

Brett opened the door and walked in, one hand behind his back. He seemed startled at my tears but came over to me. "Is that any way to greet your betrothed?" he asked.

"Good morning, Brett," I snuffled through my tears.

"What has you all in a dither? No time for tears, now."

"This lovely gown is too long. I'll never keep from tripping on it and there's no time to fix it," I wailed.

"Just put on your shoes and everything will be right as rain." He walked over to the window. "Lovely day, isn't it? No sign of rain."

"I already have my shoes on," I shouted and pulled up the skirt enough to show him one of the low-heeled slippers I had bought in London.

"Wrong ones, that's all," he said as he turned and handed me the box he had been carrying.

For some reason I'll never know, I sat down as I took the box from his hands. Otherwise I am sure that when I swooned, as I surely would have done, I should have broken another bone and completely overset the wedding. As it was, I could only look at the contents of the box and produce even more tears.

"Do you tell me that I'm getting the champion watering pot?" asked Brett.

I could only shake my head as I lovingly held up the shoes that had been in the box. They had been dyed to match the gown exactly and had little straps to keep them in place on the foot. There was a decorative buckle on the toe that winked golden in the sunlight, because of the topazes embedded there. And the heels? Ah, another example of Brett's love. They were carved from ivory and embedded with more topazes but they were fully two inches high!

With trembling hands, I reached to put them on. They were long enough but didn't seem to fit right. I stared at my feet in perplexity, then burst out laughing. I had them on the wrong feet!

When Brett observed my dilemma, he too, began to laugh and had to sit down. The aunts joined in and not to be left out, Beloved started to bark. Presently everyone in the house was in my chamber laughing, until Tyler observed Malcolm and Bessie there, at the same time, although on opposite sides and quickly threw a blanket over Mal's head.

"Sorry old man," Tyler said, "Can't see the bride before the wedding, you know," and hustled him out.

We all laughed so long and so hard that we were late for the wedding but since we were the wedding, no one complained very much.

* * * * *

It was a simple but moving service and I was not the only one who shed tears. My mind wandered occasionally as it looked forward to the day when Brett and I should be married. I wavered between joyous anticipation and absolute dread.

Bessie was supremely confident and her voice rang out through the little church as she repeated her vows. The laughter of her happiness was barely concealed in her words. I wished that all marriages could feature such a happy bride. Malcolm was stolid but equally determined and it seemed we had barely begun before it was over.

Some of the village children threw petals at the happy couple as they left the church. The barouche in which they planned to return to Hadleighwoode had been decorated with flowers by the villagers. A great cheer went up as the first marital spat was resolved by Bessie allowing Mal to drive the horses, which also had flowers intertwined with their harness. As if they too, were celebrating, they threw their heads and lifted their feet higher than usual as they pranced along.

The second barouche was for Brett and me. He handed me in as though I were made of glass and kept one arm around my waist while he handled the reins with the other. When we were out of sight of the villagers, he leaned over and kissed me and I shivered from pure exhilaration, which made him laugh.

"Our turn next," he whispered as he nuzzled my ear.

"Um," was all I could say.

As the barouches and carriages pulled up on the circled drive before the great house, the servants lined up to greet us. Malcolm started a new custom, he informed us, as he gave each servant a guinea in honor of the occasion. An extra loud cheer followed this largesse and with great jollity, we all trooped indoors.

There was to be a giant buffet and then dancing for the guests in the drawing room. At some point in the late afternoon, Bessie and Mal would slip away to begin their new life together but the celebration would continue until the small hours. Toasts were proposed and drunk to the happy couple and to nearly everyone else in the room. Brett toasted me and my face again betrayed me by turning red, which seemed to not discourage anyone. The love light in his eyes held me in thrall and I wished I could be more sure of myself.

Bessie and Mal danced the first waltz, as I danced with Harry. He was so thrilled to have been chosen as groomsman, he literally floated across the floor. I noticed however, that his eyes followed Tessa as we whirled around and around. When the music ended, Brett was at my side. I tried to move him to the side of the room where the chairs were but I might as well have tried to move Stonehenge.

"I, ah—"

"Are you tired, my love?" he asked.

"Oh no!" I exclaimed. "It's just that—"

"If you are not tired, then there is no acceptable excuse. Come." I went.

Carefully, he took the hand of my injured arm and clasped it in his. Having no choice, I placed my other hand on his shoulder just as the music began and he whirled me onto the floor.

"Bertie," he said into my ear.

"Yes, my lord?" I answered, looking down, as I had been taught.

"Look at me."

"I can't." He missed a step.

"Why can't you?"

"My, ah, feet can't see where they're going," I mumbled.

"What?" he roared. I stepped on his foot.

"Please," I whispered. "Everyone's looking at us."

"Let them look," he answered grimly. "I don't care where they look. I just want you to look at me, not my cravat."

"I can't," I repeated.

"Stuff!" he exclaimed, inelegantly and whirled me onto the terrace.

"Now please explain yourself. Why can't you look at me when we dance? You seem able to withstand such an activity at other times."

"I knew this would happen. Why didn't you listen when I said I didn't like to dance?" I asked.

"I keep remembering another 'I don't like'. Shall I refresh your memory?" I had no time to answer as I was swept into his arms and kissed soundly. When he finally released me, I stepped back and turned my back to him.

"Brett," I said in a small voice, "what drew you to me in the first place?"

"The first place?" Confusion was evident in his voice.

"Well the first time that you thought you loved me. Wherever. Why me?"

His hands were on my shoulders but I resisted the movement that would have made me face him again.

"At the Opera that night." He chuckled as he remembered.

"Yes," I whispered.

"You were so alive!"

"Alive?"

"Yes, alive and curious. Society makes such a fetish of being always bored, keeping their normal emotions buried. Gossip is the chief occupation but no one will admit to being curious or interested in anything. You truly wanted to see what was going on down there. Such an unwarranted thing for a young lady of fashion. I couldn't help but notice you."

"Oh." I walked a few steps away from him. "Did you notice me when I was sitting down, or only after I stood up?"

"And nearly fell over the edge? I don't remember. Is it important?"

"It is to me."

"Bertie, I don't understand any of this. I saw you and was smitten on the spot. I tried to get to you that night but the crowd was too thick. By the time I had reached your box you had all gone."

"But I was in London another month and you never came to call."

"I did go to see Nick the next day. He explained that you were in disgrace with Joan and might be returning to Hadleighwoode very soon. I had to go home to Ireland on some urgent business but then I came here as soon as I could."

"Why didn't you ever come to see me after you left the Army? Or write to me?"

"That's something I'll always regret. I-I let myself be talked into that foolish prank at the circus." Now his voice expressed anxiety. "Are you still overset about that? Please say you're not."

"No. I must admit that you were a very endearing beast. That at least doesn't hurt."

"Bertie, tell me how I have hurt you. I'll make it up to you every day for the rest of our lives. Trust me enough to give me the opportunity."

"Brett, I—"

"Bertie, do you truly wish to cry off? Only say that you do and I will leave you, I promise."

"I don't know."

"Do you need more time? I thought that your convalescence was the perfect time to court you. Was I wrong?"

"Except that I didn't want to be courted at all. No I believe not."

He came up behind me so softly I didn't hear him. He spun me around into his arms and looked intently into my face. "Bertie, why do you have such a fear of marriage? Are you afraid of me? Of being hurt? Please love, tell me what it is." Gently, he touched my cheek with his finger. "I can't believe that you fear me. You are such a warm and loving woman, as I know well."

"Too warm and loving?"

"No never. Just right for me. Just what I've always wanted, since that summer you were sixteen. But you have to want it as much as I do, or it won't be right. I want no woman who doesn't want me. Never have. I thought we both felt the same."

"Sometimes I do and sometimes I don't. I, er, I know nothing of such things, Brett. Of what happens with married people."

"Gently raised women shouldn't, my dear. It is the husband's place to teach his wife what she needs to know."

"But Bessie tried—"

"Oh well, Bessie. When you spend as much time in the stables as she has, you do get to see and know things."

"Will that make it easier for her?"

"I can't say. But you're not Bessie."

I couldn't keep the agony from my voice as I replied, "I know."

He tilted my head up to look at him as he said, "There really is a problem, isn't there?"

I nodded, unable to speak.

"Bertie, I promise to be very gentle with you, I promise that any pain won't last—"

"It's not that!" I blurted and turned my head away in embarrassment.

Anger shook him as he asked, "Has anyone ever, ah, did anyone try to—?"

"Oh no, or at least I don't think so."

"You'd know, I think." The tension left him as suddenly as it had appeared. "Well then, what other kind of problem can there be?" He looked around the terrace, then back at me. "Is it that you don't wish to leave Hadleighwoode?"

"I do love it here above anywhere. But I am not tied to it, as long as I could come back for visits."

"I've told you we could spend time here and you could come for visits on your own. I shouldn't mind. As long as you didn't stay away too long." Again he nuzzled my ear. "Bertie, do you love me?" he asked.

"Yes, I think I do."

"Think?"

"I've never been in love, so how would I know? I know that I like to be with you and talk to you and—"

"Kiss me?" he interrupted.

"Yes," I whispered. "That too."

"Then what can it be that troubles you so?"

"We might have children!" The words were wrenched out of me.

"I should hope so. That's one of two reasons why there is such a thing as marriage. Well, maybe three reasons."

"You don't understand at all," I wailed.

"No I don't." Puzzlement was all over him.

"They'd all be freaks, don't you see!" I tore myself from his grasp and ran back into the house.

Chapter Fourteen

ℰℴ

Tears blurred my vision as I ran back into the house past the startled guests and stumbled my way up the stairs. I shut the door to my room behind me and threw the bolt before I collapsed into my chair. I was aghast at my words. I had never meant to say them to anyone but the fear had been present since the first time I had seen Brett. I was drawn to him as I had never thought to be to anyone. At times, I had been able to overcome the fears—mostly when being kissed by Brett—but they were always there, deep inside me.

I found myself pacing my room. It wasn't fair that I should find the one man whom I could love and that he should be such a giant. Coupled with my height, I could just imagine what freaks we should produce! My brothers were all so tall that I had never realized just how far from the acceptable fashion I really was until I went to London. I knew that I was the subject of their everlasting gossip and could not knowingly subject any children I might have to such cruelty.

I was perfectly willing to accept a shorter man in the hopes of avoiding such a crisis. But then what must Nick do but accept the suit of a giant! Why wouldn't they listen to me when I said I had no wish to marry? It would have solved the problem before it began. Every time I thought I had myself under control, Brett would do something wonderful—the gown, the arm corsets, the shoes—and I would be lost again. And then there were his kisses—

A soft scratching at the door suddenly penetrated my thoughts. It was too late to be quiet in the hope that whoever it was would give up. I growled, "Go away!"

"Bertie? It's me, Bessie. Open up."

"What do you want?" I asked.

"Bertie, come help me get changed. Mal and I want to leave soon. Please come."

I went and opened the door a crack. "Did Brett send you?"

"Whatever does Brett have to do with me getting changed? Come talk to me while I get ready. It'll be our last talk as mostly unmarried sisters." She grinned and reached out her hand to me.

"And Brett didn't—?"

"Bertie, come!" She pulled me out into the hall and I looked around. It was totally empty. We hurried down the hallway to her room where she jumped on the bed and lay there, laughing.

"Oh Bertie, I'm so happy I think I'll burst! I can't wait for tonight!" At my shocked look, she gave an impudent toss of her head. "Well I can't and I'm not going to be missish about it."

She bounced off the bed and her wedding finery began to fly around the room. She giggled as one of her shoes bounced off the ceiling and came to a rest beside my chair.

"Oops! I didn't mean that." Bessie came over and looked at me. "Oh Bertie. I can't believe I'm a married woman. Who would have thought that I would ever come out of the stables long enough to fall in love? But then I didn't, because Mal found me there. Bertie are you happy for me?" She threw herself into my lap and put her arms around my neck.

"Of course, I am. What a feather-wit you are at times. But I am certain that you are the most engaging feather-wit that ever was." We hugged and kissed and the next few minutes flew by in a flurry of remembrances.

"And the best part of being a twin is that we both got engaged at nearly the same time. Isn't it wonderful?" Bessie was like a bottle of champagne, bubbling all over.

"Well, er, I don't think that Brett and I are going to, ah—"

"Bertie," she shrieked. "What have you done?"

I looked at her and could not keep back the tears. "I can't marry him, Bessie. I just can't."

"But you love him and he loves you. Why can't you?" She inspected my face. "Never say you're going to start all that rubbish about you don't wish to marry. I'll not believe it!" She shook her little hand in my face. "Not any longer!"

"I do love him, Bessie. And there is no doubt about his loving me. But I just can't—"

She looked at me intently. "You really mean that, don't you? It's not that you won't, or you don't want to but that you can't." She raised herself to the arm of the chair and took one of my big hands in her strong little ones. "Bertie we've always been closer to each other than anyone else. Please let me help you. I can't bear to see you ruin your life and Brett's this way. At least let me try?"

"Bessie, you cannot begin to imagine how horrible it was in London—"

"But I thought he said you wouldn't have to spend much time there?" she interrupted.

"No it's not that. Don't anticipate me."

"Sorry." She grinned at me.

"I was the object of so much gossip, because, of… ah, well… er, because I am so much taller than the fashion," I blurted out.

"Fustian!" was her inelegant reply.

"No really. As long as I could stay seated, it wasn't so bad. But the minute I stood up, I could see the amazement on people's faces and their eyes followed me all the way up. Then the whispers would start, like a breeze stirring tall grasses. Rustle, rustle. You can have no idea!"

"No? I suffer the other way. After I'm already standing, people expect me to stand up, so that I'll be their height. They look so foolish while they're waiting!"

"It's better to be too short than too tall!"

"Bertie you're coming it much too thick! Why do you think I ran around in boys' clothes all the time? It didn't matter in them for at least I looked like a person instead of a little doll all dressed up. Sometimes I felt that I should paint two circles of rouge on my cheeks and dance around with strings fastened to my hands and my feet, just in order to be noticed!"

My jaw dropped at this disclosure. I had never realized that Bessie might have had difficulties with her height. I was entirely too busy being perturbed about mine.

"And just how do you think I felt," she continued, "Living with a family of giants all around me? I had a permanent crick in my neck from trying to talk to any of you. At least with Mal I won't have that problem anymore!"

"No he's perfect for you. Anyone with eyes can see that," I said.

"Mal is no more perfect for me than Brett is for you, if you'd only open your own eyes and see it. Bertie, how can you be so thick?" She looked at something I could not see and in a musing voice added, "At least I can expect our children to be taller than we are, or at least some of them."

"Only some of them?" I asked. "Why not all of them?"

"Because no species breeds true all of the time."

I was startled into silence by this statement as thoughts raced around in my head.

"Bertie?" Bessie was studying me with her head tilted to one side.

There was a knock on the door. "Who is it?" Bessie called.

"It's Mal. Are you nearly ready?" he asked.

"Oh!" Bessie jumped up from the chair, her eyes wide with astonishment. "I forgot why I came in here. But you're as important to me as Mal is. He can wait a little longer." She went to the door and opened it a crack. I could hear her whispering and the answering deeper whisper of Mal. "A little while, I think," from her and, "Take all the time you need," from him. I was still lost in my confusion.

Bessie came back and again perched on the chair. "Have you been worrying about mothering a race of giants?"

Numbly I nodded. Bessie burst into laughter. "You should have listened to me sooner. I've complained so many times about trying to breed for something in particular only to get an entirely different result. It's fun, though—and at times unexpectedly wonderful—adjusting to what you get. I expect it's the same with children. Just look at the Squire's family. All sizes they are and all with different hair and eyes. And you just know that there's never been even a whisper of either of them ever looking at anyone else."

It was true. The Squire's large family was hardly ever recognized by outsiders as being just one family because of their differences—in hair color, especially. Our three brothers on the other hand were never mistaken for other than brothers because of their great resemblance to each other.

"And besides, there's no guarantee that you'll even have children. Look at the aunts." A great pang shot through me at the thought of a childless existence and I was amazed at the sense of loss that I felt. How strange that I had never really considered such feelings in my determination to remain a spinster!

"Bertie think of all the people we have known. Some unlikely families produce extra bright or extra beautiful children that one wonders where these offspring came from. We're twins and look at how different we are from each other and we should be just alike. You're so clever and musical and I'm neither! But I have an instinct for animals, while you barely know one end of any creature from the other. Don't let such a useless worry keep you from the happiness I know you'll find with Brett. Please, Bertie, don't do it!" she pleaded with me.

She gave my uninjured hand a shake to rouse me from my reverie and grinned at me. "Come help me dress. I don't want to keep Mal waiting forever. He might find someone else he likes better and I'd be forced to challenge her!"

I opened my arms to her and we hugged. "Thank you, Bessie, thank you," I breathed.

"Just go and nab Brett before he finds someone else! That's all the thanks I want. Besides I can't see you challenging anyone. You'd either slash or shoot yourself!"

To the accompaniment of her giggles, we finally had Bessie ready for her honeymoon and she was on her way, for which I was thankful. I was fretting with impatience to find Brett.

Mal was waiting for Bessie at the head of the stairs and clasping hands, they ran down together. Cheers followed them out the door and into the carriage. What an amazing little creature she was! I was grateful to have such a twin, now more than ever.

Suddenly I remembered something I wanted and went back up the stairs and to my room. I found the little box and carefully withdrew the amber key on its delicate chain. I slipped it on over my head and looked down at it lying just above the square neckline of my gown. It twinkled in the candlelight and I caressed it, making a wish in my mind.

Summoning my courage I went back down the stairs, my eyes wandering, looking for Brett. I couldn't find him. There were more people than I had remembered, but no tall golden-haired man with the smile I longed for.

Tyler was talking to the Squire. I rushed up to them, breathlessly and blurted out, "Have you seen Brett? I can't find him." My eyes pleaded with Tyler to reassure me.

"Don't think I've seen him since you came rushing through here the last time," he answered.

I hurried into the ballroom, stopping abruptly, drawing all eyes to me. I noticed conversations beginning again behind fans or raised hands. Carefully I studied every face, looking for the one I wanted. He was not there. Harry and Tessa danced by me, oblivious to everyone. Joan was glaring at me from across the room but I didn't care. Was that—? No, it was Nick, talking to someone. Mary Anne touched my arm but I shook her off, as I rushed out to the terrace and looked anxiously around.

Running from one end to the other with no success, I heard myself sob. I was beginning to panic at the thought of what I had so foolishly thrown away. I didn't know where else to look and sank down on the bench. I sat there, thumping my good hand on the bench, trying to hold back the tears when I heard a whimper at my feet.

Beloved had come to offer me her sympathy for my hurt, whatever it was. Gently she put her front feet on my knees and reached up to kiss me. I grabbed her head in my hands and sobbed, "Oh Beloved, I've been so foolish! I've driven him away." She whuffled at me her wagging tail moving her entire body.

A quiet voice behind me said, "Have you been foolish, my love?"

I should have known that voice anywhere. I jumped up and turned around to see the one I loved. I nearly tripped over the bench but he grabbed me and enfolded me in his great arms. "Oh yes sweeting, I have. Unutterably, unbearably foolish." I turned my head up for a kiss and was not disappointed. We clung to each other and I felt such peace within myself. Dear Bessie, how wise she proved to be!

Brett held me at arm's length and stared into my face. He smiled at what he saw there and said, "No more fears, I see."

"No more, my love."

"When then?"

"As soon as may be whenever Bessie and Mal come home. She must stand for me as I did for her today. Will that be soon enough?"

"Yes," he answered as he kissed me again. Beloved lay on my feet and snored quietly.

"Will you tell me, Bertie, what was troubling you so?" he whispered as he gently stroked my cheek with a knuckle. His hand dropped and touched the key resting on my breast.

"Must I?"

"No. I only wish to ensure that it will not happen again. But if you would rather not, then you do not have to. If you are sure, now, then that is enough for me."

"I am sure."

"It pleases me that you are wearing my key."

"I wish to please you as you have pleased me. I shall wear it always."

Music had again started in the drawing room and bits of it drifted out to us. "Come love, let us go tell your family that they will have another of these occasions very soon." Brett took me by the hand and led me into the house. We stopped in the doorway as he looked for my brothers. Nick was talking to the Squire now and he looked up as we approached them. We had not quite reached them when Nick suddenly grinned at us.

He shook hands with Brett and kissed me on the cheek. "I can see you've got her, old man! Think you can keep her this time?"

"What's this? The other one gone too?" asked the Squire in such a loud voice that those around us stopped talking or dancing and extended their ears.

I could feel my face beginning to turn red, as Brett answered easily, "Yes, it would appear so. Isn't that right, my dear?" I buried my face in his shoulder as I nodded.

Nick signaled to Millett and said, "Another round of champagne, if you will, Millett. We've to toast my other sister now." The old butler nodded and bowed but on his way out of the room shot me a quick smile.

Kilnarne and I passed around the room, talking to family and friends. Joan was nearly beside herself with pleasure and not a little envy I think. Mary Anne was her own dear sweet self and Brett was besieged with hand clasps and cheery good wishes.

When Millett and the footmen returned with the trays of champagne, Nick asked the musicians to be silent for a bit and invited them to partake of the wine with us. He called for silence and then announced, "It is my great pleasure to be able to inform you all that my other sister, Bertie, is about to follow in the footsteps of her twin, Bessie, whose marriage we celebrated here today. The fortunate fellow is my good friend, His Grace, the Duke of Kilnarne! Let us toast the happy couple!"

As the glasses were raised I heard someone say, "What would you expect from twins?"

And another voice said, "But they're so different!"

Brett heard this last comment and leaned down to say to me, "Thank goodness for that." I giggled.

Nick nodded to the musicians to begin again and suddenly we were in the midst of an exuberant group, anxious to wish us happy. When it seemed that my hand would break from being so shaken about, Brett looked at me and said, "I believe this is our waltz, isn't it?" The gathering fell away from us, clearing the way to the floor.

Brett took my hand and as I placed my arm on his shoulder, he whispered to me, "Look at me, Bertie." He gave me a slight shake. "Look at me!" he repeated as he clutched me more firmly.

"I don't think I can, my dear," I mumbled.

"Just do it!" he commanded. Hesitantly I raised my eyes to his. Firmly he led me out and I discovered that I was nearly floating, my feet hardly touching the floor. His eyes held mine, compelling them and with a flash of inspiration I realized why the waltz was considered scandalous and too intimate for unmarried girls to participate in. But I no longer cared about such things and I wished only that this particular waltz could continue forever.

As we circled the room, the strident voice of the Squire's wife carried to me, "Will be absolute giants, my dear."

I just laughed heartily and hugged Brett closer to me. That day at the circus flashed through my mind, when Madame Zorina revealed that each of us would have a treasure. Bessie's would be of silver but mine should be gold. Madame was exceedingly correct. As if to prove her prediction at that point, my golden treasure wrapped his arms around me and proceeded to kiss me senseless!

Why an electronic book?

We live in the Information Age — an exciting time in the history of human civilization, in which technology rules supreme and continues to progress in leaps and bounds every minute of every day. For a multitude of reasons, more and more avid literary fans are opting to purchase e-books instead of paper books. The question from those not yet initiated into the world of electronic reading is simply: *Why?*

1. *Price.* An electronic title at Ellora's Cave Publishing and Cerridwen Press runs anywhere from 40% to 75% less than the cover price of the exact same title in paperback format. Why? Basic mathematics and cost. It is less expensive to publish an e-book (no paper and printing, no warehousing and shipping) than it is to publish a paperback, so the savings are passed along to the consumer.

2. *Space.* Running out of room in your house for your books? That is one worry you will never have with electronic books. For a low one-time cost, you can purchase a handheld device specifically designed for e-reading. Many e-readers have large, convenient screens for viewing. Better yet, hundreds of titles can be stored within your new library — on a single microchip. There are a variety of e-readers from different manufacturers. You can also read e-books on your PC or laptop computer. (Please note that

Ellora's Cave does not endorse any specific brands. You can check our websites at www.ellorascave.com or www.cerridwenpress.com for information we make available to new consumers.)

3. *Mobility.* Because your new e-library consists of only a microchip within a small, easily transportable e-reader, your entire cache of books can be taken with you wherever you go.

4. *Personal Viewing Preferences.* Are the words you are currently reading too small? Too large? Too... ANNOYING? Paperback books cannot be modified according to personal preferences, but e-books can.

5. *Instant Gratification.* Is it the middle of the night and all the bookstores near you are closed? Are you tired of waiting days, sometimes weeks, for bookstores to ship the novels you bought? Ellora's Cave Publishing sells instantaneous downloads twenty-four hours a day, seven days a week, every day of the year. Our webstore is never closed. Our e-book delivery system is 100% automated, meaning your order is filled as soon as you pay for it.

Those are a few of the top reasons why electronic books are replacing paperbacks for many avid readers.

As always, Ellora's Cave and Cerridwen Press welcome your questions and comments. We invite you to email us at Comments@ellorascave.com or write to us directly at Ellora's Cave Publishing Inc., 1056 Home Avenue, Akron, OH 44310-3502.

CERRIDWEN PRESS

Cerridwen, the Celtic goddess of wisdom, was the muse who brought inspiration to storytellers and those in the creative arts.

Cerridwen Press encompasses the best and most innovative stories in all genres of today's fiction.

Visit our website and discover the newest titles by talented authors who still get inspired—much like the ancient storytellers did...

once upon a time.

www.cerridwenpress.com